SECRET VILLAGES

ff

DOUGLAS DUNN

Secret Villages

faber and faber

LONDON · BOSTON

First published in 1985
by Faber and Faber Limited
3 Queen Square London WC1N 3AU
This edition first published in 1986
Reprinted in 1987

Printed in Great Britain by
Redwood Burn Limited, Trowbridge, Wiltshire and
bound by Pegasus Bookbinding, Melksham, Wiltshire.
All rights reserved

© Douglas Dunn 1985

British Library Cataloguing in Publication Data

Dunn, Douglas
Secret villages
I. Title
823'.914[F]   PR6054.U54
ISBN 0-571-13859-4

CONTENTS

ACKNOWLEDGEMENTS

Encounter for "Women Without Gardens", "The Tennis Court", and "Wives in the Garden"; *Punch* for "Ever Let the Fancy Roam", "Mozart's Clarinet Concerto", "Photographs of Stanley's Grandfather" and "Twin-Sets and Pickle Forks".

The following stories first appeared in the *New Yorker*: "The Bagpiping People", "Bobby's Room", "The Canoes", "Fishermen", "Getting Used to It", "Kilbinnin Men", "A Night Out at the Club Harmonica", "Something for Little Robert" and "South America".

SOUTH AMERICA

Thea Docherty left Glasgow for Barlochan in September of 1937. She rented a house on the outskirts of the village. With two children, and no husband in evidence, she was a subject of talk from the day she arrived.

"What age is she?"

"Young. In her twenties. Nice-looking woman."

"And no man to be seen about the place? He must be in the Army, or at sea."

"Maybe she's a widow."

"Oh dear, don't say that, Mrs Barclay. Perhaps her husband's coming on later."

"Leaving her to contend with a move? And to look after a pair of toddlers as well? No, her man's cleared out. That is, if she's married at all."

Jack Docherty was a mining engineer, just beginning his career. A company with interests in Brazil recruited him in 1935. He talked about it with Thea, but Brazil seemed to her unlikely and exotic. She was unable to take it seriously. People like her never went to South America, and nothing would bring her to feel that Jack Docherty was any different.

"We're a wandering profession," he said, announcing that he had accepted the offer. He was gently spoken, introspective, and self-assured. "We have to think about the money," he said. "It's only for two years." When that failed to satisfy her, he became angry – not loudly, but with a faint tremor in his voice that accused Thea of failing to encourage his ambition. "Opportunities don't grow on trees! There's nothing interesting for me here in Scotland. Two years of good experience in Brazil will pave my way, Thea. Please, try to think of the future."

Jack went to South America on his own. Early in 1937, he wrote from South America to say that his employers had offered to promote him to Senior Site Supervisor if he would agree to renew his contract for a further three years. Thea wrote back that she wanted him to come home. By May, Jack admitted that he intended to stay in Brazil at least until 1941.

"With one more promotion," he wrote, in his formal but not unaffectionate manner, "I shall be in a position to bring you and the children to Brazil, where we can live very well. This is a country of limitless opportunities for a man with knowledge and ability."

Thea answered that she was sick of living in a tenement in Glasgow, sick of climbing stairs, sick of her neighbours, and sick of having to explain to people where he was and what he did. "Janet was six weeks old when you left, and to all intents and purposes she's never seen you. Alistair says 'Daddy' to strangers in the street. He doesn't remember you. Come back to Scotland, Jack Docherty. Your family needs you." She added that she was planning to find another place to live, near her family home.

Thea had been to Barlochan several times as a child, for she was brought up in Castle Stewart, a town a few miles away. Her father sent Thea information on suitable houses to rent in the district. She went home for a few days, and chose the Barlochan house.

"Don't you think it's a bit too big?" her father asked.

"It's cheap at the price," she said. "A Senior Site Supervisor can well afford it. I intend to be comfortable."

Everyone knew everyone else in Barlochan, not just to look at or to talk to but by family history stretching as far back as handed-down memories can go. From snippets of information passed on by shopkeepers, or those who had spoken to her in the street, they soon knew a bit more about Thea Docherty.

"If her husband's in South America, then why's she in Barlochan?" one woman asked. "I mean, Barlochan, of all places? They're the first new family in Barlochan in ten years."

"She comes from Castle Stewart. Her maiden name's Masson. Her father has that shoe shop in Graham Street, down the road from the British Linen Bank."

That Thea was nearly, if not precisely, local reassured the people of Barlochan. They could understand why a woman whose husband was overseas preferred to live closer to her parents. "Why not in Castle Stewart itself, though, when her man's away like that?" the woman persisted, suspiciously. "There's something wrong somewhere."

Thea was friendly, and became popular. Local people approved of her dutiful and good-humoured propriety. She visited her parents and they visited her. Alistair and Janet were neat, clean, and well behaved.

"Off for a few days this time, Mrs Docherty?" asked Mr Crichton, the grocer, who stepped out of his shop when he saw Thea at the bus stop with luggage. Alistair, who was five and a half, stood on one side of her, and Janet, nearly four, held Thea's other hand.

"It seems a bit silly," Thea said. "Heading for Castle Stewart with two suitcases."

"Mr and Mrs Masson keeping well?"

"Fine, thanks."

"The postie showed me the Brazil stamps, so I know you had a letter from Mr Docherty the other day. It's amazing, isn't it, that a letter should come all that way and arrive safe and sound? Everything still all right out there?" the grocer asked.

"He loves his work," Thea said.

Thea timed her visits to her parents to coincide with the arrival of her money from Jack at the Castle Stewart branch of the British Linen Bank. This time, though, Thea would stay for one night with her parents before leaving Alistair and Janet in their care and going up to Glasgow for a few days.

"Are you sure you're telling me the truth when you say you're going to visit a friend?" her mother asked – aware of Thea's husbandless days going by.

"Roberta Morrison's expecting me." Thea saw that her mother considered herself deceived. "Why would I lie to you, Mother?"

"There's bad feeling between you and Jack." Mrs Masson sounded relieved that she had managed to say what had been bothering her for months. "Don't deny it. It's nearly four years he's been there, wherever it is. Brazil," she said, sounding the name as if it stood for failure. "The man couldn't be content with nuts and coffee. He has to *go* there. Two years, that was his promise." Her anger at Jack's faithless

13

word seemed to be directed at Thea. "It'll be six years by the time he gets back."

"It's the money," Thea said defensively. "And it's his work, Mother. I wouldn't have married Jack if I hadn't known he'd a bit of get-up-and-go. He worked hard at night school. He's a mining engineer. He's trying to make a better life for us."

"I hope it's worth it," Mrs Masson said, bitterly. "All that loneliness for you and hard work for him."

"Don't think I don't miss him," Thea said, "because I do. But I've got to have some kind of a life, Mother, even if it's no more than a visit to a friend like Roberta once in a while. She's been down to stay with me and the children at Barlochan whenever she could, and she's been asking me for ages to go and see her."

Thea had met her schoolteacher friend at a French class in Glasgow years back – before Alistair was born. Roberta was red-haired, vivacious, rather plain, and still unmarried; she was devoted to teaching children and to attending evening courses.

"Why are you brushing up your French if you don't ever want to go to France?" Thea had asked.

"I wouldn't have the nerve," Roberta answered. "I've started Italian, too. And don't ask me – I've no intention of going to Italy, either. You know what Italians are like – worse even than Frenchmen. Or so I've read."

In Roberta's favour were the politely animated soirées she threw once or twice a year. Most of her male friends were ex-classmates from university or the teacher-training college, and most of them were spoken for. Those who were unattached seemed to have decided that Roberta was a good sort but definitely not their type.

"It feels like a hundred years since I was at one of Roberta's parties," Thea complained to her mother.

"Does Jack know these people?"

"Yes, he used to go with me. I'm dying for some decent conversation."

"It doesn't sound like Jack's sort of company," her mother said.

Thea knew she was lying to herself – that she was going to Glasgow for more than Roberta's company. She blamed Jack for the enticements of a betrayal she did not want to commit. She resented having been made to feel unnecessarily sour. Almost four years without Jack had given her more than an unwanted independence. Each additional month of separation made clearer the sense that she had been neglected and deserted. It worsened until it became an inner rancour that she tired of disguising by small talk exchanged on the streets of Barlochan, or by pretending to her mother that Jack's ambition was more admirable than selfish. The thought of Jack tinkering contentedly with machines in Brazil maddened her. She pictured him supervising workmen in the mine, in a landscape she could not imagine, or spending his evenings poring over geological data and in technical conversations with other absent husbands.

War was a month off when Thea decided she had no choice but to tell her mother she was pregnant.

Mrs Masson said nothing at first but continued with the washing-up until it seemed she could no longer bear the noise of the crockery in the basin. Drying her hands, she said tartly, "Who's the father? Roberta Morrison?"

Mr Masson was outside talking to a neighbour at the foot of the garden beside the compost heap. "I don't have the heart to tell him," Mrs Masson said. "You can't stay in Barlochan. It's a small place. They'll make your life a misery. Do you know what you've done?" Mrs Masson was angry and puzzled, indignant that no appropriate emotion showed on her daughter's face. "You might at least apologize to me, no matter what you're planning to tell Jack. Why? I never took you to be so stupid as to – So why?"

"I wanted another baby," Thea said.

Thea wrote to Roberta Morrison: "Come down if you can. It'll be your winter holidays. You can hold my hand. I don't know whether to laugh or cry, but I'll make my mind up when the baby's born." Staggered by the news, Roberta choked on her scandalized decency and on Thea's jaunty style. But ' heeded her friend's call and went to Barlochan, where Ivor was delivered by the local midwife in Thea's house. The war was four months old.

"You'd think one more baby in the world wouldn't make

15

much difference," the midwife said to Roberta, "but there'll be blue murder when Mr Docherty gets back. I know Mrs Docherty's father." Mrs MacBain held out a foot and pointed to a sensible shoe. "I bought these in his shop. She told me she just wanted another baby. Did she tell you the same?"

"Whatever she wanted," Roberta said, "we know what she's got."

"What'll I say to Mr Masson the next time I need to buy a pair of shoes? 'How's wee Ivor?' The man's face'll drop at my feet. Well, I'll away and break the news to gossips worse than me. Dr Geddes'll come and see them in the morning."

Roberta stayed for two weeks. "I wish you'd think about moving, Thea. I feel their eyes on me when I go down the street here. "How's Mrs Docherty?" "Mother and baby doing fine? Oh, that's good." It's not what they say; it's the way they say it. They make me feel like I've done something terrible. It must be worse for you."

"If I could put up with it while I was carrying the baby," Thea said, "I can put up with it now he's been born. They won't forget, but they'll get used to it. They aren't such bad people."

"How can you be so charitable when you know perfectly well how they talk behind your back?"

"I like it here," Thea said decisively, "and I see no reason to leave."

"What about Jack? What about the war?"

"Will you shut up about the war? I'm sick of it!"

"It might prevent Jack from getting home," Roberta said. "Even if it doesn't – Well, I suppose it doesn't matter now. It's all over between you and him, that's for sure."

"I don't see why," Thea said.

"Thea! How can you write and *not* tell him?"

"I need the money he sends," Thea snapped.

"Are you serious?" It had been a strenuous few days for Roberta. She was unused to childbirth, in any circumstances. She thought of Thea as her closest friend – long-suffering, indomitable Thea, who had given up on patience and allowed Jack's absence to change her. "I never thought I'd hear you say that."

"You're feeling guilty," Thea said, "because you introduced me to Ivor's father. I'm sorry. I shouldn't have reminded you."

16

"I imagine he'll join the forces," Roberta said, speculating romantically on the disappearance of Thea's lover into the vastness of life and time.

"He's just the type," Thea said sardonically.

"Do you know him well enough to be able to say that?" Roberta said, defending the father of Thea's child.

"He struck me as a decent sort. Don't you feel bad about him? Thea, you involved a perfectly decent, nice man in the ruin of your marriage."

"He's as decent as I am," Thea said. "I don't blame you if you object to having to keep a secret. But if anyone's to blame because I got lonely enough to find someone else, then it's Jack Docherty – Jack who isn't here, Jack who's been in Brazil for four and a half years. I've life left in me yet and I intend to live it, Jack or no Jack."

"But I thought you still loved him," Roberta said, helplessly. "Don't you – in spite of everything?"

"I do," Thea said, surprised that she should be questioned. She lifted the baby from its cot and unbuttoned her blouse. "I do," she said.

Women in Barlochan suspected that Ivor's father might be a local man. Thea was confronted by their qualms as she waited for Alistair outside the school gates in the huddle of mothers whose children had no older brothers or sisters to escort them home.

"Take it from me, ladies, I don't make dirt in my own midden. I go away to do things like that. All right? So the next time you see me at the bus stop with a suitcase," Thea said, casually defiant, "you'll know I'm off on the razzle-dazzle. I probably won't be, but you'll say I am."

"Mr Docherty due home soon from South America?" Mrs Munro's voice rode impishly on her question.

"I'm afraid not," Thea said. "Mr Docherty will be down the foreign mines for some time yet, chipping rocks with a wee hammer, no doubt."

"I'm dying to ask you," Mrs Gillespie said, rubbing her hands. "Do you think you'll get away with it?"

"God forbid that babies should ever be against the law!" Thea said laughingly, and the women laughed with her.

"I was meaning when your man gets back," Mrs Gillespie said seriously.

"If I were to let you in on my secret, you'd tell everyone else, Mrs Gillespie, and then you'd all be at it. Society round here would go to pot! No, I couldn't live with the responsibility."

She knew she had given them something to laugh at. There were no broken marriages in Barlochan, although these women were familiar with marriages made elsewhere than in Heaven, some of them their own. They looked at Thea, wondering if she was stupid or very brave. She knew she had also given them a chance to say behind her back, "She'll laugh on the other side of her face when her man gets home, when he steps off that bus and sees her pushing a pram."

Letters from Jack took longer to reach Barlochan now, and came at irregular intervals. A few arrived stamped "Delayed by Enemy Action". Sometimes her replies included snapshots of herself, Alistair, and Janet. She gave him news of their progress. She mentioned all the local characters without mentioning that she had become one herself. Each time she wrote to Jack, she went once again over the question of whether to tell him about Ivor. In imaginary conversations with him, she explained her simple motive: "I wanted another baby and you weren't here." She accused him of selfishness. "What do you expect if you stay away for six years? I used to say to myself, Jack Docherty, that if you'd any family or friends you wouldn't have stayed away from me all that time. You'd have had more to call your home. But that doesn't say much for me, does it? How do you think I feel when I read out your messages to Alistair and Janet: 'Be a good child and do well at school and look after Mummy for me'? I don't feel proud, Jack."

Thea's misgivings demanded that she keep Jack in ignorance for as long as she could. The family could never do without the monthly payments he sent.

"There's war work in Greenock," Thea remarked to her parents. "They're looking for women to train as machinists."

"You?" her father said. "A machinist for the war effort? And Greenock's miles away!"

"I don't give a damn for the war effort," Thea said. "I need something to do."

"What about the children?" her mother asked. "Ivor's too

young to be left with us."

"You're right," Thea said. "God forbid that I should do a Jack Docherty on them. It just crossed my mind."

"If you're needing a change," her father said, "why don't you go up to Glasgow and see Roberta?"

"If I did that," Thea said, "Mother would think I was off on a fertility spree."

Mrs Masson thought about it. "I can trust you not to be daft twice," she said.

When Thea got home to Barlochan that day, there was a letter from Jack saying that he would be staying on in Brazil until the war ended. She read and reread the letter for suitable signs of sorrow or regret, but gave it up as a waste of time. Jack described at length the responsibilities of his new position as Regional Engineer. Thea went to Glasgow with one purpose in mind.

"A man, a big-hearted man, might forgive or get used to one spare bairn about the house. But two – no, no, two's enough for a man not to feel safe," Mr Masson said, between groans of worn fortitude. "I used to think you were the most sensible girl I ever met. That last time, I took a blow. I really did. And now this. You're not even upset! Same as last time – not so much as a tear in your eye." He was puzzled by Thea's composure. "You should be ashamed, but you aren't. You ought to be scared stiff, but I don't see any signs of that, either."

"Why should I be ashamed? I wanted another baby, and I'm going to have one. Did I ask Jack to go to South America?"

Her father waved at her to stop. "You'll have to write and tell him," he said. "It isn't honest to leave a man in such terrible ignorance."

"You mean he deserves to know. All right, I'll tell him," Thea said. "As soon as I've given birth."

"Thea," Mr Masson pleaded, "go and console your mother. Behave to her as a daughter should in your position. Give her at least one hint of shame or remorse for her to hold on to."

Edward was born in April 1943. Mrs MacBain brought Dr Geddes with her, but the midwife's hunch that the birth might be difficult proved wrong. Dr Geddes had nothing to do but urge Thea to push, while Mrs MacBain shouted back at him, "What do you know about it?"

Thea was half asleep with exhaustion and relief when she was awakened by the sound of Dr Geddes's voice talking to Roberta and Mrs MacBain in the next room. "It's a load off our minds that there aren't too many servicemen stationed round here. Otherwise, Mrs MacBain and I would be bringing more little strangers into the world with fathers not properly accounted for."

"We had one a fortnight ago," Mrs MacBain said, nudging Dr Geddes's memory. "Mrs Archibald, two years wed, and her man in the Navy. He was away less than a year – eleven months and a week, for I added it up – and then his wife drops a daughter."

"Old Mr Archibald came in to see me," the doctor said. "He was wondering if there was such a biological fluke as an eleven months' gestation. Eighteen months in elephants, I told him, nine in the human female."

"What was that?" Thea shouted from the bedroom. "Mrs MacBain! Who's that you're talking about?"

"You should be resting," Mrs MacBain chided.

"Did I hear you say that Sheila Archibald gave birth?" Thea asked, pugnacious with happy surprise.

"You'd have heard it sooner or later," Dr Geddes said, "but don't tell anyone you heard it from me. Her folks are trying to hush it up."

"I wondered why I hadn't seen her. The slut!" Thea said with satisfaction. "And her man in peril on the high seas. He'd hardly turned his back on her – disgusting!" She laughed.

"Oh, Thea, how can you be so cock-a-hoop at a time like this?" Roberta said, appealing to Dr Geddes and Mrs MacBain to support her low opinion of yet another scandal.

"Now, now," said Dr Geddes, "we mustn't distress Mrs Docherty. You must be very tired," he said to Thea. "You should be resting."

"Tired my foot! I'm jubilant! Poor, loyal Roberta. I don't think you'll ever understand me," Thea said. "I'm proud. I'm really proud of this one," she said, kissing her new baby. "You'll have a wee friend," she told him. "Someone just like you."

Thea stood on the step before the teller's elevated wooden counter in the British Linen Bank. "The manager would like a word with you, Mrs Docherty." The teller pointed to the glassed-in office.

"I'm sorry, but these monthly drafts have been curtailed," the manager said.

"Is it the war?" Thea asked. She was frightened, but she had known it was only a matter of time before she had this interview with the bank manager.

"It could be a new currency regulation introduced by the Brazilian banks. Wartime does that," he said. "I've written to Glasgow to find out." He looked at a document in the file before him. "So far, my instructions are that Mr Docherty's standing order in your favour is now in abeyance. We should receive clarification in a few days."

"Does it say 'until further notice'?" Thea asked.

"No. Can you think of a reason why it might be cancelled?"

"I can think of a couple of excuses," Thea said, "but I can't think of a reason. Can you recommend a good lawyer?" She wondered if she was serious, and decided that she was.

She had half expected it since she wrote to Jack introducing the existence of Ivor and Edward. Still, his indirect but practical answer was a shock.

"I know that in the eyes of everyone except me I've wronged Jack Docherty," she told the lawyer, Mr Birnley. "But he started it. He wronged me first by going to South America. All right, I accepted two years, even with two children to bring up. I indulged his career. And eight years have passed! South America!" she shouted. "What sort of place is that to be when his wife's here, and Germans and God knows who else could've been baying at my door? I feel his wrong to me day by day and week by week."

"And yet it's no fault of Mr Docherty's that you now have four children to bring up."

"I've been trying to explain just that!" Thea said.

Birnley was intrigued by her combativeness. He was familiar with the human habit of taking the offensive to excuse one's criminal or immoral act, but he could not recall coming across a

21

woman who asserted devious justifications with such barefaced poise. It was his experience that women clients were often timid. Imminent litigation and its formal authority awed them; their tongues were humbled by proximity to the great institutions of respectability and truth. Their limited vocabularies stuttered into attempts to prove that they were good at heart. Guilty or not guilty, they usually wept, but he felt you could always see when a woman was telling the truth. Thea's rugged aplomb amused him, as did the challenge she posed to his skills.

"The news about little – ah, Ivor," he said. "Well, news of that sort, coming straight out of the blue – I mean, Mr Docherty might not want to . . . " Whatever he meant to say vanished in gestures. "You may be asking too much of him if you expect him to understand, to forgive, your moral or instinctive lapse . . . your little error, Mrs Docherty. Two little errors, Mrs Docherty, two – yes, to be candid, two contraventions of your marriage vows. Why didn't you write to him sooner?"

"I didn't see any point in worrying the man unnecessarily," she said. "It's not easy to explain a thing like that in a letter. You think about it. And what's this about lapses? Errors? I never did anything I didn't intend to! I might be all too human, but I'm not a fool."

"I find myself quite able to understand your husband's feelings," Mr Birnley said, leaning across his desk and using his sternest gaze to probe Thea's character.

"Feelings be damned! It's a thoughtless husband who'd stay in Brazil for as long as he has and then cut us off without a penny. Two of the children *are* his, in case you've forgotten." She looked at the lawyer with grave determination – so closely that he had to turn away. "Are you trying to wriggle out of a case you don't know how to turn down?" she demanded. "Are you trying to work out whether you can afford it? All I'm asking is that you write to him and point out the dire consequences poverty might have on his children, Alistair and Janet. Take a note of their names. I'll fend for the other two." Her tone challenging, she said, "Don't imagine that I'm irresponsible."

"That's reasonable enough," Mr Birnley said, without conviction.

22

"Too reasonable!" Thea said. "I've compromised."

"A fair man recognizes reason when he sees it," the lawyer said.

"Oh, is that a fact?" Thea said ironically. "And tell Jack Docherty I'm willing to have him back, in spite of what he's made me do."

"You want Mr Docherty – You want *me* to ask Mr Docherty to come *back* to you?" the lawyer asked slowly, dwelling on his bewildered emphases.

"I want to live in a house with a man in it," Thea said. "*My* man. I made my bed, and I'll lie in it, given half a chance."

Six months went by and there was no answer to the lawyer's letter. "He may not want to reply," Mr Birnley suggested. "There's also the uncertainty of the wartime mails. Ships are sent to the bottom and planes are shot out of the sky. These are daily occurrences, Mrs Docherty. For all we know, there may be an embargo on your husband's leaving Brazil, especially to attend to – not unimportant business, I grant you, but personal. Mining is an essential industry. Ores," he said, speaking to Thea's simmering impatience, "make metals, which go into ships, guns, tanks, planes. Your husband may well be considered indispensable."

"Don't talk to me about ores! I know more about ores than you do."

Barlochan noticed that Thea Docherty had less money to spend. She sometimes asked the grocer for credit. Women had often remarked that Thea's children were the best turned out in the village; their reputation for perfection began to dwindle. Mr Masson gave Thea money, but not much, or often enough, and she was too proud to ask for more. She wrote to the welfare department in the government offices at Castle Stewart. Someone was sent to see her.

"Your house seems a little on the large side," said the official, a middle-aged woman whose eyes roved professionally around Thea's living room. "Couldn't you find something smaller, less expensive to run?"

"I've four children," Thea said.

Thea told her how Jack had gone to South America in 1935,

and of the punctual monthly payments that had stopped almost a year before.

"Nineteen thirty-five?" the official asked, her eyes weighing up the room as she underlined that date in her notebook. "Ivor's such a lovely, unusual name," the woman said to Thea. "I seldom come across it. I take it that Mr Docherty's at least managed to get over on leave a couple of times?"

"Unfortunately," Thea said, "Mr Docherty's been too deeply involved in the South American economy."

"I see," said the official. "Then that's almost nine years he's been away?"

"He was very, very good at writing to me," Thea said, slyly.

"I can see that a rather remarkable correspondence has been taking place; I can see that for myself." The woman closed her notebook with a decisive slam. It sounded like a door closing. "Frankly, I don't believe there's all that much we can do for you, Mrs Docherty. Money's awfully tight, and there are so many cases of hardship at the moment. The best I can promise you is that your case will come before the board in due course. We'll let you know." She stood up. "Personally, I feel that a smaller house would make a big difference to your circumstances."

"You're standing there thinking I've got myself into a right mess, aren't you?" Thea said aggressively.

"It's not for me to judge. I see so many different cases. It's water off a duck's back to me."

"But you *are* judging."

"Only in the sense that I doubt if my department would take this case very far. You have quite some way to go before you would qualify as a charge on what little funds we have for poor relief."

"You look as if you're eating something delicious, and far too good for the likes of me," Thea said. "No, I'll drop it altogether. I'm sorry I bothered you."

Thea went to work in her father's shoe shop, taking Ivor and Edward with her each day to Castle Stewart and bringing them back on the evening bus. "I'll do anything," she said, "but I won't give up my house, Jack Docherty or no Jack Docherty."

Roberta came down as often as she could, and one

24

November day she and Thea took the children to the coast, a few miles away. They walked along the beach as the wild, grey wind swept in over the sea. "You're a teacher, Roberta," Thea said. "You should know. Which way is South America?"

"That way," Roberta said, after a hesitant pointing that stopped when she felt she had the direction right. "Really, I don't know. I think it's that way." Thea looked along the line of Roberta's arm. "Ireland's blocking your view!" Roberta shouted as Thea took Edward from his pram and walked closer to the sea. "You aren't looking straight at South America!"

"Ireland be damned!" Thea said. "Alistair! Janet!" she shouted. "Come and look at South America!"

There was no news of Jack until the war was over by almost a year. Mr Birnley called Thea into his office to show her a letter he had received from a solicitor in London. It said that Mr Docherty, of the Southern Hemisphere Mining Corporation, no longer wished to communicate with his wife, and that in view of her repeated infidelities he felt under no obligation to contribute to her financial support.

Mr Birnley made clicking noises with his tongue, waiting for time to pass. He pulled a handkerchief from his pocket and blew his nose, his eyes fixed on Thea as she studied the solicitor's letter. "He's being very harsh," he said. "I expected the offer of a sum for Alistair and Janet. We'll pursue it, of course."

"No, don't," Thea said, still rereading.

"We'd be better placed to demand provision for Alistair and Janet if you were to commence divorce proceedings," Mr Birnley said. "I doubt if the court would sympathize with your attitude to two additional children born out of marriage," he said. "But Mr Docherty's prolonged sojourn in Brazil can be considered in two phases. First from 1935 to the conception of little Ivor, and the second after that event. Please, don't interrupt me," he said, his hand waving to hush Thea's protestations. "I know your views on this subject. But I must advise you of the best legal tactic. That first stage of absence was a long one, involving a broken promise to you. There's a case there. His obsession with his career in South America contributed greatly to the wreck of a marriage which a little

25

consideration for you could easily have saved. I can hear a first-rate lawyer make an excellent argument out of that." He looked pleased. "What do you think?"

"I think he's still in South America," Thea said.

Thea wrote to Brazil and told Jack that she had no intention of initiating a divorce, and that if he took the first step she would fight it until everyone believed that his selfishness was to blame for all that had happened. There was no answer. She wrote again: "You can come home now, you stupid man. If it's your pride that's been bothering you, surely to God there's been enough time for your wounds to have healed." It was like talking to the night sky.

"You should stop believing that Jack'll come home, walk through that door, and forgive you," Roberta said in 1950. She was visiting Barlochan again, this time to interview for a post in the local primary school. "He's been gone for fifteen years! Are you sure you'd recognize him? How could you live together after all that's happened?"

"I don't even like him," Thea said. "Roberta, you've loved my children and you've brooded over me. You've been a great help, a lovely friend, and I'll always be grateful. But you still think I've got what I deserve, don't you?" Her tone was quiet but exasperated and disappointed. "You think that I was reckless and impatient, that I didn't 'wait' for Jack. Well, I did and I didn't. More did than didn't, in my opinion. If you're going to come to live here, I ought to know what you really think of me."

"I haven't got the job yet," Roberta said.

"And being Thea Docherty's friend won't be the best recommendation in Barlochan."

"I don't know about that," Roberta said. "I'm not sure what I think about you, and, if you ask me, the people round here don't know what to think, either. But I've spent a lot of time here, and now and then I get the feeling that they actually admire you. I suppose I do, too. After all, I haven't had a very exciting life. So far," she said, touching wood. "The best part of it may have been your . . . well, I don't know what to call them."

"Mistakes?"

26

"As a candidate for the post of headmistress of Barlochan Primary, I ought to call them mistakes, or worse. But no – I wouldn't let anyone call Ivor and Edward 'mistakes'."

At her interview the next day, the school panel, which included Dr Geddes among other local worthies, questioned Roberta at length on her views on primary education, and seemed pleased with her answers.

"Excellent references," the chairman said, leafing again through her file.

"Thank you," said Roberta.

"We understand you have connections in Barlochan," he went on.

"Yes," she replied. "An old friend, Mrs Thea Docherty." She looked at Dr Geddes, who smiled at her. She took a deep breath. "I ought to say that if I get the position I'll be moving in with her on a permanent basis. Her house is large, even with four children, and we've been friends for a very long time." She felt herself to have been challenging and strong, perhaps for the first time in her life. But her spirited declaration didn't so much as raise an eyebrow. It was all water under the bridge.

"Thank you, then. We have two other candidates to interview, and we hope to reach a decision tomorrow morning. Will you be at Mrs Docherty's?"

"Yes," said Roberta.

Dr Geddes winked at her, and gallantly escorted her to the door.

"Ah," said a panel member. "I see you've done extensive study in Italian language and literature. I work with a committee for the repair of war damages in Pisa." He leaned to look at a fellow-Italophile on the panel.

Roberta was embarrassed to speak from the door. "I'm afraid I've never been to Italy," she said. "The war . . . "

"One day you really must – particularly with your interest in Italian. Well, it's been a pleasure."

Dr Geddes winked again, and closed the door behind her.

"So much for local scandal," she said to Thea the next day, when she was offered the job. "I'm surprised – stunned. They must have been able to tell just by the look of me that Barlochan Primary's in no danger of exposure to moral turpitude."

"Aunt Roberta, did you ever meet my father?" Alistair asked one day.

"Yes, long ago. Several times. The last time I saw him, Janet had just been born."

"If you want to know about your father," said Thea angrily as she entered the room, "then you ask *me*."

"I have asked you."

"And I've told you. The sooner we forget that scoundrel the better."

"Then why did you write to him at Christmas?" Alistair said. "I saw the envelope before you posted it. In Castle Stewart," he told Roberta, "so the Barlochan postie wouldn't know her business."

"Thea!" Roberta said. "Did you?"

"Well, it was Christmas," Thea protested quietly. "I sent him a Christmas card."

Miss Frame returned from the till carrying a gentleman's change on a plate. She placed it before him and he thanked her. He did not hand her a tip. In the tea-room behind Arnot's Bakery tips are left discreetly on the table, beside saucers or plates.

Little has changed in Arnot's Tea-Room in the twenty-four years Miss Frame has worked there. It continues to hold its own against the eateries, pizzerias, Cantonese restaurants, curry shops, self-service sandwich bars or the little restaurants with foreign menus and rubber-tree plants that have been opened by energetic young graduates. A concession to economics has been made in that a cashier no longer sits on her high stool inside the varnished cash desk, knitting between her responsibilities; but the cash desk is still there, the tables are in the same positions and they are the same tables. Linen tablecloths have yet to be usurped by plastic, washable surfaces and the cutlery is the same heavy tableware it has always been, bearing the name Arnot, like the white, robust crockery.

Middle-aged, traditionally suited men from local businesses, legal and insurance offices and the County Buildings form the body of Miss Frame's lunch-time regulars. Women who have come into town to shop are to be seen recuperating in Arnot's with a salad, avoiding the standard fare listed on the small, typewritten menus, those steak pies, beef olives, roast beef, chops and fish in batter (Fridays only) which are relished by Miss Frame's gentlemen. These dishes go under the description of "special business lunches". They begin with soup and end with Apple Crumble or Rhubarb Tart and a large jug of custard.

Arnot's cakes, scones, cream cookies, tarts and crumpets are well known in that town. You can buy them in the shop you have to pass through to get to the tea-room. Old ladies turn up for afternoon tea and sit two or three to a table around layered cake stands. "We'll just have a selection," is a favourite order, made to sound as if it is not too much and not too little. "Two of each." The entry of a laden cake-stand, held high from the ring at the top, is a sight to make weaklings or the abstemious choke on their modest scones. Once placed on the table a cake-stand looks like an object of worship. It looks like a Babylonian castle of calories. Taking their time, these dignified old gluttons dismantle the heap of cakes, layer by layer, licking their fingers and wiping their mouths on the linen napkins.

Miss Frame supervises these scenes. Teaspoons chink against china, confidences are whispered over raised cups. She supervises them, as if from a great height, with maximum competence, stiff courtesy to strangers and a smile which rounds out her cheeks to those she knows. Her greying hair has never been seen ruffled; she has never been known to sweat, panic or lose control. No heel has come off her black shoes, no stocking would dare to ladder on her legs during the hours of work. She is composed, in charge, full of figure but tall, broad-shouldered and solid with it.

"Where d'y' think these old women put them?" Maureen asked, holding up a despoiled cake-stand. "Ugh! Aw that cream! Aw that sugar! Ugh! I couldny eat like that, Miss Frame."

"Just you be grateful, m'lady, that they're eating at all. It's guzzling old madams who keep us in a job." Bad table-manners appal Miss Frame; but over-consumption is among the dining-room phenomena she is used to. Her customers tilt their plates of Scotch broth away from them when they come to their last spoonfuls of that nourishing soup. They do not suck soup off their spoons. Most of them desist from speaking with their mouths full.

For fifteen of her twenty-four years at Arnot's, Miss Frame has been manageress. She no longer wears a white apron over her black skirt and matching twin-set. The absence of an apron, the presence of her artificial pearls – "No, Maureen, it's *me* who wears the pearls" – announce that she is in a position of authority.

"Y' know," said Maureen, "if she w's to order us to wear the starched linen cuffs, an' the wee white frilly lace tiaras, it wouldny surprise me. Aw this place needs is Max Jaffa an' an aspidistra."

"An' thigh-length black skirts, black stockings wi' the tops showin', an' high-heels, Maureen?" Mandy suggested, almost as if she liked the idea.

"Y'r brains 've got housemaid's knee," said Maureen.

"How many twin-sets d' y' think she has?"

"If she hears y', she'll have y'r guts f'r suspender belts."

"Maureen!"

"Yes, Miss Frame?"

"A jar of mixed pickles for Mr Gregory, and with the silver pickle fork, if you please."

"Yes, Miss Frame."

"The silver pickle fork? That Mr Gregory's been let inty the club, an' him only comin' here f'r two years Maureen," Mandy said, with bantering disbelief.

"I'll gi'e 'm a curtsy," said Maureen.

Miss Frame has lived on her own for almost two years. Her son works in Manchester. Her flat is at the top of a red sandstone tenement block. Her neighbours have known her for too long to be bothered to refer to her as an "unmarried mother". Miss Frame's age, apart from anything else, has led them to forget about her mistake or misfortune. Years of her upright, dominating politeness on the communal stairs (which Miss Frame scrubs cleaner than anyone else), on the landings, or at the bus-stop, persuaded her neighbours of her respectability. It was not always like that. It is a good neighbourhood and they wondered at first what she was doing there and how she could afford it. Miss Frame did without in order to afford it. She was determined her son would get the chance he deserved. She used to notice her neighbours looking at her as if they were trying to decide if she was an abomination or an admirable, self-sufficient mother, and coming to the conclusion that perhaps she was an admirable abomination. She cleans, sews, knits, reads and listens to the wireless.

"Ma friends think I'm a joke," said Maureen, "'cause I work here. 'It's good training,' ma mother said. Aye, f'r wh't? I said. I can lay a table, carry plates, smile nice at auld men who ca' y' by y'r name wi'out bein' asked, an' I'm heart-sick o' meringues."

"D' y' think y' could ever get like her?" said Mandy,

nodding to where Miss Frame was talking to one of her regulars.

"It's the way she leans over them. Y' know? That way she h's o' speakin' to th'm while she stacks th'r plates. She respects that lot somethin' rotten."

"Don't you believe it," said Maureen. "It's aw an act. She's as hard as nails."

In the dead hour between two and three, Miss Frame goes out. On certain days she goes to the factor's office and pays her weekly rent. On another day she goes to the insurance office and pays her weekly premium on the policy on her life. She goes to offices where she pays her bills for rates, gas and electricity. Her money has always been organized like that: so much for this, so much for the next thing, so much for that, and nothing left over.

She used to think that when her son grew up life would be easier. Extra money has not compensated her for the loss of his company. But the humiliations of the past are long over, those arrangements she had to make with a neighbour, for their older boy to bring her son home from school and keep an eye on him until she got home herself. Or the things she could never afford. Or the detested allowances and the official prying and form-filling she had to go through to get them. Or the way her neighbours would talk to her about the effort to make ends meet and which she felt sure was different from how they spoke of commonplace difficulties among themselves.

"That Mr Cruickshank!" said Maureen, exasperated.

"And what's he done now?" Miss Frame asked, amused.

"I wish to God he wouldny hold ma hand every chance 'e gets. Miss Frame," she appealed, "it gives me the creeps."

"You tell me," she said, "if he ever makes a real pass at you." Miss Frame has a wise tolerance for the familiarities of her regular customers. "And Mr Cruickshank, or no Mr Cruickshank, he'll go out that door as if he had wheels on his shoes."

"He holds ma fingers an' strokes ma hand. Y'd think 'e w's a fortune teller. Know wh't 'e did last week? 'This little piggy went to market'," Maureen enacted on her fingers, "'an' this little piggy stayed at home, an' this little piggy . . . ' I kid you not, Miss Frame. On y'r bike, I said. Y'r no' goin' up ma airm!"

"Middle-aged men like to be served by attractive girls," said Miss Frame. "That's one of the reasons why they eat out." She likes to pass on her experience. "It's also one of the reasons why we employ you."

"An' here w's me," said Maureen, "thinkin' I w's a waitress, but it turns out I'm the Co-op Undertaker's wee whore."

"Maybe," said Mandy, "we should ask Mr Cruickshank out, an' gi'e 'm the scare o' 'is life. Is that no' an idea, Miss Frame? We'd rub 'is body wi' meringues an' then clear off wi' that black suit o' his."

"That's enough of that, m'lady," said Miss Frame. "And *I'll* take Mr Cruickshank his steak pie."

"An' if 'e strokes y'r hand, Miss Frame?"

"If he strokes my hand," she said, "he'll get it in the eye."

"She's no' such a bad auld stick," said Maureen.

Half-past four is the time when business slackens off at Arnot's. A few women might still come in with their parcels and packages and sit with a shoe discreetly removed under the table, stretching their toes and confiding to the waitresses that their feet are killing them.

"Who's that with Miss Frame, Maureen?"

"That's wh't I w's wonderin'," said Maureen, who had watched the young man come in, carrying a suitcase. He stood with Miss Frame under the arch between the shop and the tea-room. Miss Frame was happily surprised but apprehensive. They sat down together at a table. After they'd spoken for a few moments, Miss Frame kept looking toward the door.

"Never seen 'm before," said Maureen. "Never seen her, either," she said, as a young woman came in. The young man stood up, pulling a chair from the table so that she could sit down. She shook hands with Miss Frame. They began to talk.

"D' ye think I should go over?" Mandy asked.

"You do that," said Maureen, frowning with curiosity.

"Can I get you anything?" Mandy asked.

Miss Frame reacted by pushing her chair back, as if she would get whatever they wanted by herself, or had been caught sitting at Arnot's table with customers, or took Mandy's solicitude as an impertinence. Her son asked for tea, for three, and some scones.

33

"Obvious, isn't it?" said Mandy, buttering a scone.

"Obvious wh't?"

"That fella's 'r son, and she's never met that girl before."

"Miss Frame?"

"Miss Frame must be Mrs Somebody-else, or Miss Frame's got a wee secret. Fill that tea-pot, will ye?"

"Miss Frame's more likely to be 's auntie," said Maureen.

"She w's thrown, as soon as she saw that boy. She kissed 'm, I saw it. An' that look when that girl came in? Come on, y' saw it y'rself. Interestin', isn't it?"

"Look. Gi'e me that, an' I'll take it in. You bring the tea."

"Awfully curious all of a sudden, aren't we?" said Mandy, primly bitching.

"If I left it to you, I'd find out nothin' but a load o' your guesses. I'm tellin' y', y'r terrible."

As Maureen arrived at the table she overheard the young man call Miss Frame "mother". "Lovely day," she said, placing the scones on the table, smiling at the young woman and then at Miss Frame's son.

"Don't," said Maureen out of the side of her mouth, stopping Mandy in the short corridor between the tea-room and the kitchen, "Don't call her 'Miss Frame'."

Mandy came back, beaming with satisfaction. "Wh't'd y' say?" Maureen asked.

"Said it w's a lovely day."

"Aw, no, that's wh't I said. But y'r right. He called Miss Frame 'mother'."

"Told y', didn't I?"

"Y' forgot the sugar."

"Deliberate, wasn't it?" Mandy said, picking up the sugar bowl. "Silly me, Miss Frame. I forgot the sugar."

"Don't act it!" Maureen said angrily.

"There's somebody else in," said Mandy when she came back. "You go or it'll look suspicious, an' I'll hover." Maureen left. "An' Maureen? Keep y'r ears open."

Maureen heard the young man say to his mother that he had forgotten his keys. Miss Frame said she'd get hers from her handbag. Maureen went after her into the small staff cloakroom. She leaned at the door, her arms folded, watching Miss Frame rummage in her bag.

"Nice lookin' fella," she said. Miss Frame glanced at her, unable to be angry or show any concern that what she had managed to keep from Arnot's for years had been discovered.

"You run awfy deep, Miss Frame." She walked past Maureen. "If somebody'd told me, I wouldny 've . . . " Miss Frame did not stop to listen.

She gave her son the keys, and went out to the pavement with them. She waved after them as they walked away.

Passing Mandy on her way to the kitchen, she said, without looking at her, "You come in here, m'lady."

Maureen and Mandy waited for what Miss Frame had to say. "I don't want you two talking about me," she warned. "Not in here, and not to anyone. I couldn't stand it. All I'm asking," she said, "is that you keep it to yourselves." She sat down and looked up at them.

"These women in the shop areny daft, Miss Frame."

"If they ask you, then say that you don't know."

"It comes as a bit of a shock," said Mandy, teasing her.

"He came straight up here from Manchester," said Miss Frame, "to tell me he's engaged. And she came with him." She took a white handkerchief from her black sleeve.

"Wh't else did y' expect?" said Maureen. "A nice fella like that, Miss Frame. It's what he would do."

"Does she know?" Mandy asked.

Miss Frame nodded, Yes, and dabbed an eye.

"Don't worry about us," said Maureen. "We'd like y' to know, wouldn't we, Mandy? We'd like y' to know th't this makes y' just one o' the girls. Isn't that right, Mandy?"

"I couldn't take it," Miss Frame said, "if these women who work in the shop were to know about me."

"Sure, sure, we'll no' tell. B't wh't I will say is this, Miss Frame." Miss Frame looked up at Maureen. "If you don't nick this, an' take it home wi' y', or at least get rid o' it," she said, putting the silver pickle fork in front of her, "then I'll tell everybody, b't everybody. Right, Mandy?"

"It's the pickle fork," said Miss Frame.

"That's right. It's the pickle fork that no' everybody gets to use. It bothers me. An' that's ma price. Get rid o' it."

35

WIVES IN THE GARDEN

Every year, in the same week of August, we visit our old friends Malcolm and Henrietta Blair at their summer house in Kintyre. We off-load our children on their grandparents and the Blairs do the same.

Within half-an-hour of arriving at the house, Malcolm and I invariably find ourselves looking at the ocean. It is, he claims, the best view of the sea you can find, whether from the west coast of Europe or the east coast of America. He is very proprietorial about his view of the Atlantic.

From where we stand on rough, salty grass, the house is about two hundred yards behind us. Turning round, we might catch sight of Laura and Henrietta, watching us from a bedroom window. They have conversations of their own, as they unpack our suitcases.

"I can stand here," I said, "look out there, and I find it hard to believe I'm actually in Europe. It's a feeling of precariousness, Malcolm. I feel I'm at the extreme edge of a continent."

"You haven't changed, have you?"

"Why do you say that?"

"Because," he said, "you sang a similarly sentimental aria last year."

Malcolm has a condescendingly elegant smile. He is a university lecturer. An amiably long-suffering expression in the face of untenable points of view is a trick his profession has perfected over centuries. "But give or take a Hebrides or two, or a few rocks, it *is* the edge of Europe. Still the same old Steve," he said, contriving to make me feel how tall he is. "Still unrealistic and pushing forty."

"You said that last year, too."

"Did I?" he said, casually pointing to cormorants, those black birds which fly towards the sea like caricatures of thirst. "I dare say I'll say it again next year."

In spite of the two unused cups which we saw were waiting for us on the coffee table, Malcolm went straight to the half-empty shelf among his bookstacks where he keeps his whisky. He poured two glasses, one of which he gave me.

"Other people's libraries," I said, "always look much more impressive than mine."

"This is the only place where I can work." Bookshelves filled an entire wall. There were piles of books on the floor. On a desk, by the window, there were more books. Most of them were place-marked with strips of paper. Signs of academic industry were everywhere.

"We had to hire a van at the beginning of the summer," Henrietta said. "And I counted them. He shipped a hundred and ninety books. You'd think that was enough, wouldn't you?" She looked at Laura. "Oh no, he's on the phone to the university library at least once a day."

"Once," Malcolm corrected her. "Once in seven weeks." They eyes met. Their subdued anger made me come to Malcolm's assistance. I'd hardly opened my mouth when Henrietta interrupted.

"Go on, then," she said. "You were ecstatic enough when you dug them out, and you said you were dying to show them to Steve. So go on, then. Why don't you?"

"Show Steve what?" I knew their voices, their expressions, well enough to understand that Malcolm was trying to outwit Henrietta's seriously teasing tone with pretended innocence.

"You know what," she said.

"Does Laura speak in riddles?" he asked me, in his best superior manner. "Henrietta does."

"Malcolm!"

"When you ask her where something is, she says 'In there' without pointing. In where? 'Upstairs, in the drawer.' Do you know how many drawers we have, upstairs?"

"Malcolm!"

"Another drink? Girls?" he coaxed.

"Didn't you hear us laughing?" Laura said, looking at me, the one who knew nothing.

"I dug out," said Malcolm, hesitantly, as he poured, "some old school photographs. And I apparently shouldn't have done that." He continued pouring, his back still turned to us. "I remember you saying you'd lost yours."

37

"They're probably upstairs," I said, looking at Laura, "in a drawer."

"No they aren't," she said. Why are women so powerful? "They're in that box in the attic, beside your school blazer, your prefect's badge, your tie, your running vest, and your running shoes with the withered grass on the spikes." Why are women so accurate? They remember everything.

"Laura! That's rich! Oh, Steve, why? Why have you kept all that stuff?" Henrietta gloated.

"Why?"

"Come on, Malcolm!" Laura demanded. "Show him the photographs!"

"I will," said Malcolm, coolly, handing out drinks. "I will, later."

"Now!"

"Why now, for God's sake?"

"Because," said Henrietta, "we want to watch you looking at them."

"Well," I said, clapping my hands, an irritating habit of mine which Laura hates, "I think I'll go for a stroll."

"Sit down, you coward!" said Laura.

Henrietta reached over to the table beside her. Malcolm's photographs were sinisterly convenient. "Malcolm," she said. "Be a dear and pass these to Steve."

Malcolm had to cross the room to take the photographs from Henrietta. There was the hint of a snatch in how they came into his hands. Or was it a thrust from the other side? "Thank you, darling," she said, keeping one picture back, over which she and Laura began to titter.

"There's Fat Moffat," said Malcolm. He sounded disappointed, saddened that the sentimental pleasures of reminiscence had been ruined. "And Nimmo, Napier, Anderson."

"No," I said. "That's Nimmo, and that's Napier." An insolent grin, hovering over a shadowy pallor, stared out from the formal ranks of seventeen-year-old boys. Hair oil glowed on short hair.

"We can go over them later," Malcolm whispered. "There are

38

faces I can't put names to. There are faces here I don't even remember."

"Steve!" said Laura, holding up a picture of the relay squad. One boy held the baton like a truncheon. All four runners looked happy, half-naked and breathless. "And that's you!" Henrietta laughed. She doubled up with mirth. A half-melted floe of ice slid from her tilted gin. "What lovely knees you had!"

"Pull up your trousers," said Henrietta through the spaces in her jocosity. "Go on, pull them up. I want to see your knees."

"You've seen my knees."

"Not for a whole year I haven't. Pull up your trousers."

One way to thwart this teasing, I thought, is to play them at their own game. I pulled my trousers up over the knees and walked round the room with as much flaunted theatricality as I could manage. "I may have put on weight," I said, "but you have to admit it, I've kept my legs. And my neck," I said, raising my chin, "I've kept my neck." Malcolm blinked with dismay.

"But your best feature," said Laura, "is your feet."

"Really?" said Henrietta. "Take off your shoes, Steve."

"I will not. I draw the line. What's caused this?"

"Yes," said Malcolm, unsure, I thought, if he should risk the question, "what's at the back of all this?"

"And can you," asked Henrietta, ignoring our questions, "still touch the ground with the palms of your hands? You were very proud of that."

Knowing my tactics had been soured by superior forces, I bent over as vigorously as I could. They knew I was stupid, but they would see that if nothing else I was still reasonably fit. With a groan that was more sincere than I'd intended, I touched the varnished floorboards with the butts of my hands. "Can you do that?" I said to Malcolm, blaming him for everything.

"I wouldn't even try," he said, quickly pouring himself another drink.

A long time ago, when touching the ground with the palms of my hands didn't rip the fat off the backs of my legs, we were waiting for Laura and Henrietta in a spaghetti restaurant.

They arrived, studiously late, without apologies. They, too, were students.

Whatever values of the spirit the Beat Generation possessed were re-embodied in us as bare feet in sandals, itchy beards, stretched sweaters and a conspicuous lassitude. Laura and Henrietta imitated the fashions of the time. They wore black wool stockings, black polo-neck sweaters, skirts with wide belts and large buckles, anything, especially their hair, or their Gauloises, which made them look like Juliette Greco in downtown Glasgow. They were up-market in looking that particular part. There was nothing improvised or scruffy in their appearances, which made us look lucky, as if we did not deserve such nice girlfriends. If they liked to carry copies of *Evergreen Review*, which we loaned them, it was not because they appreciated their contents. Neither did we, much, but we said we did. We entered into serious haggles for books of poetry published by the City Lights Bookshop – San Francisco! – which could be bought second-hand from strangers "passing through".

That afternoon Laura sat and sulked. She stared from one table to another like a distressed vamp. I was worried about her. "Why don't you eat?" I said, as she turned the plain pasta over with her spoon. "It's awful, but it's costing Malcolm all he's got left." She scratched her breasts with casual deliberation as she looked at people at other tables. Her sweater was a tight fit. From the visual point of view, what she did to it was of considerable fascination. "I don't think," I said, "you should do that."

"What of it?"

"That man there, he thinks you're making a pass at him."

"And what if I am?" Her look of contempt was so effective I thought she must have rehearsed it in front of a mirror.

"Please," I said, "don't do it."

Malcolm put the photographs away. I was sitting with my drink, my trousers still rolled up above the knees. "Poor Caroline," said Henrietta. "She's a mouse. She sits at home daring herself to have a second dry sherry. She hates that rugby crowd. Laurence knew it before he married her. She knew it. Honestly, I don't know why they bother."

"Remember?" I said to Laura, drawing her attention, and

pausing until everyone was quiet. "That day, in the Continental, when I told you off for scratching your nipple?" There was a shock, a turbulence of raised eyebrows. Laura and Henrietta filled it in with laughter. They were laughing so much that day it was beginning to make me nervous. "I don't know why you're laughing," I said to Henrietta, trying to be firm. "*You* used to call yourself *Hank*." If anything, they laughed louder.

"What made you bring that up?" Laura asked.

"Nothing," I said, closing the subject. "It just entered my head. I just remembered it."

"For heaven's sake, will you roll your trousers down!"

"Up, down, make up your mind, woman! Shall I take them off?"

"No," said Henrietta. "I wouldn't do that."

In parts of the world where summer really is Summer, men must be more familiar with the agreeable sensation of seeing their wives walk out of the ocean than is possible in Kintyre. Few arrivals of the woman you love are as contenting as seeing her run towards you across the sand, having swum, splashed and waded in the sea.

Idle talk on the beach while our wives are in the water is an occasion of summer calm that has become an indispensable part of that indispensable week. Malcolm sits on his chair, wearing slacks, a formal shirt with one button open at the neck, shoes and socks. I lie on the sand in my swimming trunks.

"The sea's really a kind of garden. That's why women look so much better in it than men do. It's no coincidence we have mermaids, and naiads, or that Aphrodite was a woman."

"What about mermen?" I said. "Not to mention Neptune or Poseidon, or whatever you call him."

"Did you see Henrietta slap that wave?" he said. "It took her by surprise. My God, she slapped it, as if it'd been naughty. More plonk?"

"Later," I said. "I think I'll take the plunge."

"Be a merman, then." He always professes contempt when I decide to go in for a swim.

"It's freezing!" I shouted as I splashed around the shallows.

"No it isn't," said Henrietta.

"What?"

"You can't be cold," she said, "because I'm not."

"You've kept your neck, darling," said Laura. "But you're sadly deluded about your legs."

"My legs are as they always were."

"Your legs," said Henrietta, "are a disgrace, unlike," she said, "mine."

"We've decided," said Laura, the sea breaking across her belly, "that we've kept our looks so much more successfully than you or Malcolm. Haven't we?"

"Can't you persuade that slothful medievalist to come down to the water?" Henrietta asked.

"If you can't," I said, "then how can I?"

"Let's swim out a bit," said Laura. She and Henrietta swam out to the calm deeps, knowing, I think, that my feeble, untutored strokes would not take me that far.

One late afternoon, we noticed our wives had gone out into the garden. Both were wearing wide-brimmed white hats, those elegant shirts they make themselves from expensive material, and long skirts. Clearly, when they changed, they had no intention of gardening, but that was what they were doing. They knelt on a rug at the edge of a flower bed and they were weeding it, conversationally. A concession to the earth had been made in that they wore white canvas gardening gloves. Dropped leaves were sprinkled on the brim of Laura's hat. "They haven't changed much," I said, "have they? They were fashion-conscious when we first met them. Looking back, I think we've always been 'accessories'." Why do we gloss over love like that, using a tone of voice which we don't mean? Wind blew a birch leaf upright on the brim of Laura's hat. It stood there, balanced like a high-diver before it blew away.

"Yes," Malcolm said. "Lately I've felt myself as a sort of handbag, or walking-stick."

"Walking-stick?"

"An accessory."

"Does Henrietta carry a walking stick?"

"You know what I mean," he said, crossly. "An accessory."

"*Walking-stick?*"

42

"Do you think," he said, "that if we put our best suits on, they might allow us to join them?"

We watched our wives through the open French windows as they plucked and picked at what few weeds were growing in the flower beds. They were talking, but too quietly for us to overhear. They worked slowly, the way our mothers do over their needlework and knitting when they meet on weekday afternoons in a rotation of houses, over their secret conversations.

"Actually," Malcolm said, "I remembered that day in the Continental, but I didn't want to say anything." He got up and stood discreetly behind the blowing curtains at the window. "I remember it very clearly. I remember what she said, too."

"Said what?"

"'It *itched*.'" He laughed quietly. "I was impressed."

"She didn't say that. I don't remember her saying that."

"I'd come to the conclusion that women have a different kind of memory," he said. "But yours, yours is just faulty."

"Women," I said, "have a clearer sense of irony, but my memory," I emphasized, "is perfectly vivid as far as that day's concerned."

"'It itched.'" he repeated, with a chuckle.

"She didn't say that."

Laura sat on her heels and stretched her back. Henrietta copied her. We stepped back into the room, afraid of having been caught in the act of looking at our own wives. For some reason we had to keep it secret. It was the kind of embarrassing experience that makes you look at your watch.

"All week," I said, "I think they've been playing up on our bad faith. Thank God they haven't got round to remembering the phrase."

"Bad faith?" He laughed the laugh of the unjustifiably incredulous.

"We're too guilty of how we've changed," I said. "All we do is disguise our bad faith to ourselves."

"Bad faith? *Mauvais foi*?"

"*Mauvaise*. Arrogantly enough, it's feminine."

"What," he asked, "became of Napier? It's *important*. What's

43

Fat Moffat doing? How many kids has Nimmo and do we *know* who he married?"

"I don't care what happened to Napier. Come to think of it, I didn't like him then, and I've gone right off him now."

"All summer," he said, downing his drink, "I've been realizing how I've spent years trying not to be middle-class average. But now," he said, "I want my destiny." He bent over his hugged glass. "I don't want to be different any longer."

"Malcolm, you were never *very* different. You're inventing yourself."

"Last week, I saw people playing tennis. They were our age. I never played tennis in my life and neither did you. But I watched them, wishing I knew how to play, and saying to myself, 'Wouldn't it be nice? Wouldn't it be nice to play like that, with Henrietta, and Laura, and Steve?'"

"You used to think these people who lived for the tennis club were despicable."

"When we should have been playing tennis with nice middle-class girls in short skirts, what were we doing? We were swanning around dives talking tripe about Jean-Paul Sartre in two languages. In your case, in three languages. What are you laughing at now?"

"I've just seen a vision. Of you, playing tennis. Eighty degrees in the shade, and Malcolm Blair serving. White slacks and sensible pullover. You *never* wear shorts!"

"I stood at the French windows again. For all of five minutes I was on my own, watching our wives. Malcolm joined me there. He topped up my glass from the bottle. "They've been cutting flowers," he said, almost pathetically.

Laura's tight-fitting gardening gloves were bulged on the finger on which she wears her rings. In the dark, inside the glove, I imagined them shining with commitment and convention. Esther Reids, Sweet Williams, late cornflowers, the last of them for the year, were bunched in her arms.

"Why is it?" I asked Malcolm. "Why do I respect women so much? I like them much more than men."

"Why not? After all, most of them are so much taller than you are."

We sat down together on the sofa. "In Gaelic," Malcolm

44

said, "the name of this whisky means 'heaven'."

Our wives came in through the French windows carrying their flowers.

"What's for dinner?" Malcolm shouted roughly. He shouted like a man angry at having been kept waiting, when, in fact, he had drunk so much whisky he thought it was later than it actually was.

"Do I," said Henrietta, "detect signs of strain?"

"They've been arguing," Laura said.

"It's *him*."

"Shut up," I said to Malcolm, giving him a push. "I'm going to ask them. I'm going to ask them what they think of us."

THE CANOES

Peter and Rosalind Barker began their holiday on Loch Arn on an evening in the first week of August. We were standing by the rail of what is known in our village of Locharnhead as the Promenade – a name that does no more than repeat the intent of the old Duke, who paid for its construction many years ago as a means of employing our fathers. It is just a widening of the pavement by the side of the road that runs along the head of Loch Arn and then peters out in an unpaved track a mile farther on. We have ten yards of Promenade, and that is not much of a walk. Our fathers used to lean on a low stone wall there. Now, as the old Duke considered this wall a symbol of our fathers' idleness, the job of knocking it down for good wages was meant to be significant. As a boy, I remember the old Duke's rage when, within a day of the work's completion, as he found our fathers loafing on the splendid new barrier they had just built, he craned from the window of his big car and cursed them to lean perpetually on a hot rail by the hearths of damnation. On summer evenings, therefore, we stand where our fathers stood, and one or two very old men sometimes stand beside their sons. For the most part we keep our mouths shut and enjoy the mild breeze that whispers across the water.

The Barkers looked a prosperous young couple. Mr Barker could have been no more than thirty years of age; his wife might have been a year or two younger. Their skins were already tanned, which I thought strange for two people at the start of their holiday. Mrs Barker wore a broad red ribbon in her fair hair, and I was pleased to see that her husband was not the sort of young man whose hair hides his ears and touches his shoulders. They both wore those modern clothes that, in my opinion, look so good on young, slender, healthy men and women. And I noticed that they wore those useful shoes that have no laces but can just be kicked off without your stooping to struggle with ill-tied knots as the blood rushes to your head.

Mr Barker parked his car in the place provided by the County Council, adjacent to the jetty. The jetty was paid for by the old Duke. It is announced as Strictly Private Property on a wooden notice board, though few people here can be bothered to read notices. The paint has long since peeled from it, and its message is rewritten in the badly formed letters of the new Duke's son's factor. Perhaps more would be done for the attractions of Locharnhead, which stands in need of a coat of paint throughout, if it was not the sort of place you can only get back from by returning along the arduous way you came.

Our eyes swung genially to the left to inspect the new arrivals – all, that is, except those of Martin MacEacharn, who is so dull of wit he proclaims himself bored with the examination of tourists. They are a kind of sport with the rest of us. Much amusement has been given to us by campers and hikers and cyclists in their strange garbs and various lengths of shorts and sizes of boots. We tell them they cannot light fires and pitch their tents where they are permitted to do so; and we tell them they may light fires and pitch tents to their hearts' desire where gamekeepers and bailiffs are guaranteed to descend on them once it is dark and there will be no end of inconvenience in finding a legal spot for the night.

Young Gregor remarked enviously on the couple's motorcar. It was low to the ground, green, sleek, and new, and obviously capable of a fair rate of knots. Magee, whose father was an Irishman, ambled over toward Mr and Mrs Barker, pretending he was too shy to speak to them. They were admiring the fine view of the long loch from the jetty. Mr Barker had his arm around his wife's shoulders and was pointing to various phenomena of loveliness in the scenery. They are a familiar sight to us, these couples, who look and behave as if they feel themselves to have arrived in a timeless paradise of water and landscape and courteous strangers in old-fashioned clothes. On fine summer evenings the stillness of the water may be impressed on all your senses to the abandonment of everything else. Our dusks are noted far and wide and remembered by all who have witnessed them. On Loch Arn at dusk the islands become a mist of suggestions. There are old songs that say if only you could go back to them once more, all would be well with you for ever.

Mr Barker noticed Magee beside him and said, "Good evening," which Magee acknowledged with his shy smile and slow, soft voice. "You'll be looking for me, perhaps," Magee said. All of us leaning on the rail of the Promenade – Muir, Munro, Young Gregor, MacMurdo, MacEacharn, and myself – nodded to each other. When the couple saw us, we all nodded a polite and silent good evening to them, which we believe is necessary, for they have heard of our courtesy, our soft-spoken and excellent good manners and clear speech. All except Martin MacEacharn extended them the thousand welcomes; he was undoubtedly thinking too hard in his miserable way about the Hotel bar behind us and for which he had no money to quench his thirst.

"If you're the boatman, then, yes, you're the man we're waiting for," said Mr Barker to Magee. My, but he had a bright way of saying it, too, though we all thought that a couple who possessed two long kayak canoes on the trailer behind their motorcar had no need of a boatman. He towered over Magee, who is short, wizened, bowlegged, and thin, though his shoulders are broad. Mrs Barker, too, was a good half foot taller than him.

"Well, I think I can just about more or less manage it," said Magee, with a quick look at his watch, which has not worked in years. "Yes," he said, for he must always be repeating himself, "just about. Just about, if we're handy-dandy."

"Handy-dandy?" said MacMurdo with contempt. "Where does he pick them up, for goodness' sake?"

Magee, as we all knew, was desperate for a bit of money, but a lethargic disregard of time is obligatory in these parts. Or that, at least, is the legend. What I will say is that if Magee is late for his dinner by so much as half a minute, his wife will scatter it, and probably Magee as well, before her chickens. Social Security keeps him and the rest of us alive, and I have yet to see a man late for his money. If it ever came to the attention of the clerk that Donal Magee turns a bob or two with his boat, then he would be in deeper water than the depths of Loch Arn, some of which, they say, are very deep.

It soon became clear why the Barkers couldn't paddle themselves out to Incharn. Gear and suitcases are awkward to transport by canoe. Magee, a lazy man, turned round to us with a silent beckoning. He was asking us to lend him a hand but was frightened to say so aloud for fear that our refusals might ruin the atmosphere of traditional, selfless welcoming he had created with such skill and patience. We turned away with the precision of a chorus line it was once my good fortune to see in one of these American musical films – all, that is, except Martin MacEacharn, who wasn't looking.

Once Magee had loaded his boat and tied the canoes to its stern, the flotilla set off in the dusk like a mother duck followed by two chicks. I treated them to one of my lugubrious waves, which I am so good at that no one else is allowed to make one while I am there. How many times, after all, have the holiday types said to us, "We will remember you forever"? It is a fine thing, to be remembered.

Incharn is a small and beautiful island. That, at any rate, is how I remember it, for I have not stepped ashore there since I was a boy. A school friend of mine, Murray Mackenzie, lived on Incharn with his mother and father. Only one house stands there among the trees, with a clearing front and back, between the low knolls at each side of the small island. When the Mackenzies left for Glasgow, or whatever town in the south it was, Murray was given a good send-off at school. We had ginger ale, sandwiches, and paper streamers. The minister of the time presented him with a Holy Bible, in which we all inscribed our names in their Gaelic forms.

For a good few years the house lay empty. None of the Duke's men were inclined to live there and put up with rowing back and forth on the loch to get to work and come home from it. A childless couple took its tenancy. The man was a forester, and every day he rowed his boat to a little landing stage by the loch side and then followed the steep track over the hill. But his wife was visited by another boat, at whose oars sat Muir's elder brother, a self-confident and boastful lad who had spent four years at sea with the P & O Steam Navigation Company. Still, the poor woman must have been lonely on Incharn, all by herself most of the day, and she would have grown sick of it, especially in winter, waiting for her man to row back in the early dark; and it would have been worse if there had been a

wind blowing or a bad snow. Muir's elder brother went back
to sea without so much as a farewell to his fancy woman, and
he has never been heard of since. She was found by her
husband, standing up to her middle in the waters by the
pebble beach, shivering and weeping but unable to take that
last step – and one more step would have been enough, for it
shelves quickly to the depths. They, too, left, soon after that,
and the island and its house lay empty. To row past it used to
give me the shudders. I was a young man then, and had been
away, and would go away again.

For a number of years the house has been rented in the
summer months. The Duke's factor will accept only those who
are highly recommended by the solicitor in London who
handles the Duke's English business.

Magee and his hirers were soon no longer visible to the naked
eye. We lounged by the rail, which has been rubbed by our
hands and elbows to a dull shine. Muir, I think, remembers
his lost brother when he looks toward Incharn, though he is
too sullen to say so.

"Another couple to Incharn, then," said Munro. "Now,
there's been more folk through the door of that house in a
couple of years than there have been kin of mine through the
door of my mother's house." He always calls his house his
mother's. She has been dead for twenty years; but we are born
in houses, as well as of mothers.

"It's a sad thing that no one will lend a man the price of a
pint of beer," said MacEacharn.

"If we wait for Magee returning," said the cool, calculating,
and thirsty MacMurdo, "then we'll have the price of several
apiece. A twenty-minute drag over the loch is worth a pound
or two."

"Aye," said Young Gregor, "and don't forget the twenty
minutes back."

Eyes tried to focus on Incharn as its form vanished into the
dusk. Lips were wetted by tongues as we imagined the pints of
beer to which Magee might treat us on his return if we behaved
nicely toward him or threatened him with violence. But Magee
was in one of his funny moods. He is not the man to stand
up to a woman like his wife. Munro has said, "I'm glad I am

married to the woman who accepted my proposal, but I'm doubly thankful I'm not married as much as all *that*."

Magee did not come back but illustrated once again how he has inherited from his father an aptitude for the evasion of responsibilities. He beached his boat a few hundred yards to the right of us, where there is a spit of sand, and then went home in the dark with his money, hoping perhaps to buy a few hours of peace and quiet through giving his wife a cut of his boatman's fee.

That Magee had been well paid is a matter of which I am certain. A couple of nights after the arrival of Mr and Mrs Barker, I had nothing to do, and Magee agreed that I go with himself and another English couple to Inverela, where there is another house on the new Duke's son's estates. It stands by the loch side and cannot be reached by road unless you park a mile from it and then walk along a narrow track. To go by boat is only sensible.

"Well, well, then," Magee began as we were taking our leave of the Englishman on Inverela's tiny landing stage. His wife, by the way, was running around cooing about how wonderful it was, but we took no notice of that. "I hope the weather stays fine and the loch remains as calm as a looking glass all the while you are here." Highly impressed by this eloquent desire for their comforts, the Englishman gestured for his wife to come over and hear this, because it was obvious that Magee was far from finished. "And may there be no drop of rain, except perhaps once or twice in the night, to make your mornings fresh and to keep the leaves as green as you wish to see them." They settled back before this recitation. "And may your sleep be undisturbed and tranquil and you have no reminder whatsoever of the cares of the world, which I am told are the very devil outwith of Loch Arn. And, to translate from our Gaelic" – of which Magee knows one curse, two toasts, and a farewell – "may your bannocks never freeze over or your hair fall out, and may you never forget to salt your potatoes."

I imagined how that couple would say to each other, as soon as our backs were turned, that it was true after all: the people here speak better English than the English. In that matter, the explanation is to be found in the care with which our kinsmen of long ago, in their clachans by the shores of Loch Arn, set about forgetting their original tongue so that their children, and their children's children, and all their posterity would converse in translation.

As Magee stepped into his boat, it was in the way of a man who expects to be paid nothing at all for his troubles. His grateful employer was shuffling in his jacket for money – a sight studiously avoided by Magee's little blue eyes, which are too close together. The Englishman had a look of prosperity about him and a willingness to be forthcoming. "Ah . . . ah . . . " The Englishman was a bit embarrassed. "How much do I owe you?"

Now, there can be a long and historical answer to that one, but Magee thought for a moment with one hand on his chin while the other removed his hat and began scratching his head. "How . . . how much would you say it was worth?"

"Would a fiver do?" said the Englishman. His wife nudged him. Magee, like myself, was quick to notice that this woman, in a hat of unduly wide brim – dressed, it seemed to me, for a safari – was a touch on the overpaying side of humanity.

I was all for putting an end to Magee's playacting and stretching my own hand out to receive the note. But Magee began ponderously calculating: "Now, then . . . It is thirty minutes out, after the ten minutes it took to get you aboard, and unloading you took another ten minutes, while it will take us another thirty to get back home . . . . "

That was a fine stroke of obscurity, for the man was nudged once more by his grinning wife, and he produced another fiver. Two fivers together was more than the government gave you for having no job. Magee looked at the notes as if insulted. "Now, that seems a lot to a man like myself . . . sir," he said. "How does the seven pounds strike you . . . sir? You see, it's the fair price."

"A bit of a problem there," said the gent. "I haven't a single note on me."

"Then, in that case," said Magee, a bit too quickly, "I'll take the ten pounds and I'll see you when you come to Locharnhead."

"How will we get there?" asked the woman, who was already blinking in a soft hail of midges.

"By that boat there," said Magee, who pointed to a beached rowing boat that belonged to the house. "Or you may walk by the track, on your right."

"Ah. I see. Yes, indeed. On the right, you say?"

"On the right, sir. But you will be quicker by the loch."

I remember it took the Englishman four hours to row to Locharnhead the following day, for that canny son of an Irishman had been to Inverela that morning to hide one of the oars. Magee did well with a sort of contract for their subsequent transportation.

"Ten pounds for a night's work, Magee," I said on our return voyage. "Is it not a liberty to take so large a sum, even from an Englishman who looks as though he can well afford it?"

"Do you want a drink?" he asked. "Or do you want a *good* drink?"

"You know me," I said.

"Then hold your hush and don't whine at me for a hypocrite. Because daylight robbery is exactly what it is, and you and the rest of them will sup on the benefit of it. Though I'll tell you true enough that if he didn't look such a pig of a rich man in his pink shirt and white breeks, I'd have let him off with the three pounds the factor says is the fixed charge to Inverela."

We passed Incharn on the return trip in the late dusk. I waved to its holiday tenants, who had lit a fire on the beach. That couple we'd just left at Inverela could not be imagined lighting a bonfire. I had a feeling the Barkers would have been glad of our company if we had called on them for a few moments, but the thirsty lads, we knew, would be waiting for us on the Promenade, and with me in the boat Magee would have no chance of getting up to his tricks. In the light of their bonfire Mr and Mrs Barker looked like people of the far long ago, when, we are told, there was great happiness and heroism in the world. Or it may just have been the way they carried their youthfulness that led me to think so.

"Now, I hope you didn't fleece that nice couple of the Barkers there."

"What kind of a thief do you take me to be? I asked for the factor's fixed charge, and they were kind enough to pass me a fiver."

"Aye, well, there will be no more work for you out of that pair. These two are water babies."

A day or two later I was walking on the hill. My old pal Red Alistair was, I knew, reluctantly laying down a drain on the Duke's lower pastures – the one he was meant to do the year before but didn't get around to finishing. He is called Red on account of the political pamphlets he inherited from his father. He is annoyed by the nickname, being twice the Tory even than the new Duke's son, and he keeps his legacy of pamphlets in deference to his father's memory. As I was looking for Red Alistair, I found the minister scrutinizing the loch through his spyglass.

"Now, there's a sight I've never seen on the loch before," he said. "There are two canoes on it today."

He gave me his glass and I had a clear view of Mr and Mrs Barker in single line ahead. They wore yellow waterproof jackets and sensible life jackets as well, which was a relief to me.

"Is there any chance of that becoming popular?" I asked the minister, after I had told him who the two canoeists were and what nice people they had turned out to be.

"You should ask that of Young Gregor. He's the boy who's daft on boats round here, though if he ever opens that marina he does nothing but talk about, we will become a laughing-stock for our broken craft, and make no mistake."

He was as disappointed in Young Gregor as we all were. "Go, for God's sake, to a southern city," we urged the boy. "There's nothing here but old men and the bed-and-breakfast trade." Lack of capital was what he complained of – that and the poor show of enthusiasm he received from the manager of the Bank, which comes twice a week to Locharnhead in a caravan.

"These canoes can fairly shift some," said the minister. "My, if I was young, I'd be inclined to try my hand at that. What an emblem of youth is there before our eyes."

"We should encourage Young Gregor in it," I suggested. "These craft appear to have no engines at all."

"That boy will break my heart. Is there nothing that can be found for him to do?"

"Can you imagine any woman from round here sporting about on the water like that?"

"Our women are not so much bad-natured as unpredictable," he decided. "By and large, though, it might be the bad nature you cannot predict. But we have known great joys in our time. There is no sweeter thing in this life than an harmonious domesticity. You know, I even miss the bad nature of my late wife." He paused as he peered through his telescope. "They are a tall couple, these English Barkers."

"They tell me she is called Rosalind."

"Now, that is a name from Shakespeare, I believe."

"Then it's a fair English name," I remember saying, "for a young woman as handsome as Mrs Barker and with a true demeanour to go with it."

"It makes a change from Morag, or Fiona, I'll say that much," said the minister.

For many more minutes we stood there on the hill, exchanging the spyglass as we watched the two canoes.

"What day is it?" asked the minister.

"I think it must be Thursday, for I saw the women waiting on the fishmonger's van."

Mr and Mrs Barker visited the Hotel bar in the early part of some evenings for a drink and a bite to eat. While they were inside, we took the opportunity of examining their Eskimo craft – not, of course, that there is much to look at in a kayak canoe. I studied them longer than the others had the patience for. A jaunt in one of them would have been very satisfying. To have asked Mr Barker might have been thought a bit eccentric of me, though I doubt if he would have taken it as an impertinence. Their canoes had a very modern look to them, as, indeed, had that bright and lively couple with their air of freedom.

"Aye," said MacMurdo, who joined me on the jetty, "that must be a fine and healthy outdoor sport for them – the sort of thing that could set you up for the winter and keep you well." MacMurdo, fresh-faced as he is for his years, is housebound for three months of the calendar with the sniffles. When the Barkers came back, we stood to one side and said our soft

"Good evening" together, which they returned. Then we watched them slip into their canoes and paddle away into the early dusk.

"It's the best time of all to be on the water," said MacMurdo. "Just look at the beauty of it over there. The whole world is getting itself ready to settle down for the night."

"Do you think he'd mind if I asked him – I mean, if he'd let me take his canoe out for a few minutes?"

"What's so special about one of these canoes?"

"They strike me for one thing as an exciting little sort of a craft, that's what. Now, look there, and see how close you would be to the water."

"A man of your age . . . A boat like that is for young things."

"It would be interesting to *me*."

A man like myself might be expected to resent these folks who come up from the south like the swallows to take their ease on a country that has brought me no prosperity. All the same, no one can tell me better than I tell myself that I am as lazy as any man born. Part of my trouble is that I have become content enough on plain victuals in modest quantities and two packets of Players a week. What jobs I've done in other parts than this one did not contribute much to my happiness. But there are things I've seen, and people I've met, I would not do without if I had my chance again. When the mobile library, which is a wonderful thing, calls at Locharnhead, I am the first man aboard and the last man out. That is not hard, as the only other reader in our community, apart from the youngest MacMurdo when he's at home, is Mrs Carmichael, wife of our stingy publican and the Hotel's cook. By the way, I once ate a large dinner there. It was not worth the money, and Magee and the rest of them watched me through the window for all five courses, screwing up their faces and licking their chops in an ironic manner. MacEacharn, I noticed, was there, too, but that obstinate man wasn't even looking.

But for all the large contrast between myself and the likes of Mr and Mrs Barker, it made me mellow and marvellously sad to watch them paddle in the still waters of Loch Arn at dusk, going toward Incharn, where the Mackenzies once lived, and that unhappy couple who followed them.

Incharn, as I have said, is a beautiful island. A good number of trees grow there, and on the side you cannot see from the head of the loch there is low ground and a growth of reeds of which nesting swans and water-fowl are appreciative. This is the most beautiful side of all, though you can only see it properly from the water, which means that it has been observed by few people. Facing Locharnhead, the beach is of fine pebbles, and it slopes quickly into the water. Crab apples grew there when my friend Mackenzie lived on it, and that bitter fruit made grand jelly in his mother's big copper pan. They had a black leaded stove of great size, which Mrs Mackenzie kept as spotlessly black as a Seaforth's boots, and we were famous for the spit and polish. Mrs Mackenzie would do her washing in a wooden tub on the beach, and her suds floated and spread as Murray and I threw stones at the scattering patches of foam. People on holiday do no washing at all, I'm told. Sometimes I felt like telling Mr and Mrs Barker about Incharn, but I never got round to it. They might have been interested. Magee has been known to tell those he ferries to the island of the tragedy that befell there. In his story, the woman drowned herself, and her demented husband first slew her lover with his bare hands and then committed his own life to the chill waters, but it was not that way. For all I know, the Barkers heard that story from Magee; but if they did, they were too happy to pay it any heed.

At night you can see the small lights of the cottage if its blinds or curtains are not drawn. In our famous dusks and sunsettings, the lights seem to spread in the open and watery mist, and they float above the island like benedictions. A man can look toward Incharn and feel drawn toward it. Muir's brother may have felt that, too, for whether the beauty of a place discriminates among those who are to be compelled by it is not a subtlety I am prepared to go into. Incharn draws a charitable thought from me, at any rate. But then I was always a bachelor, though not because I wanted to be one; and so I am always glad of something that holds disgruntlements at bay. All winter long I look forward to the holiday couples. It would please me more if Mr and Mrs Barker were to come back, with their frail canoes, and the way they splashed each other with water off their paddles, and capsized and rolled over under the water and came back up again as my heart beat with admiration for them – and, above all, the way they just followed each other about on the still water.

GETTING USED TO IT

Harry Boyle bumped into Vic Nairn on the corner of Hairst Street. "Harry! Now, you're a sight for sore eyes!" Nairn's cliché greeted Harry with the familiarity of something well known and detested. "Long time no see!"

"I don't go out much these days, Vic."

"It's very sad, Harry. But I understand." Nairn's thin, worn, saddening appearance disguised an iron constitution as ill-health. "Bob MacQueen was round at my house last week," he said in his slow, emphatic pronunciation, which was that of a man with a west-of-Scotland accent trying to speak "properly". "We were talking about you. There I was," he said bitterly, his lips thinning as he drew them against his teeth, "thinking I was in for a quiet night, with a can of beer, and the TV on, and the wife in the kitchen. When what happens? The doorbell rings. Down to the door, then," he said wearily. "And who's there? Bob MacQueen's there. That man depresses me. Oh my God, Harry," said Nairn in a drawled moan that he seemed to drag up from depths of bilious malice, "but that's the most miserable man I've ever met!"

"Bob isn't the most generous man I know." Harry was judicious, for Bob MacQueen was a man he placed in the same category as Vic Nairn. "And how's your health bearing up, Vic?" Nairn was a man who never said he was well.

"Not too good," said Nairn. "Worse."

"You look well."

"Do I?" Nairn asked, with the surprise of someone who thinks he knows better. "Maybe I *look* well . . . "

Harry Boyle was unemployed and, as Nairn knew, he had all the time in the world. He passed some of it taking the family dog for its walks. Having managed to get past Vic Nairn, he risked walking the beast off its little legs by carrying on down King's Road, as if walking off a heavy dinner. Entering High Street on his way home, he caught sight of Bob MacQueen approaching on the same pavement. A change in the traffic lights released a stream of cars, which prevented him from slipping unnoticed across the street.

Cursing his luck, he decided he would have to go through with it and hope that MacQueen was in a hurry. MacQueen was a plumber with his own business, and although he had known Harry for years, only a promotion to a white-collar job had made Harry a man to be spoken to in the street and fit for MacQueen's friendship. It was about four-thirty on a day in January, and the rain had stayed off, although everyone in the street was dressed as if expecting to be drenched at any minute. In one of the Co-op's display windows, bedside lamps were aglow on bedside tables. Silent TVs were on in the window next door.

"This is quite a coincidence," Harry said, forcing himself to be agreeable, tugging his terrier on its leash. It was sniffing around the shopping bag of a displeased woman at the bus stop. "I've not long been talking to Vic Nairn – "

"I ran into Vic last week," said MacQueen, as Harry hauled on the leash and the hungry dog skidded across the pavement. "He was none too steady on his feet. Drink taken, if you ask me. And it doesn't improve him any. But then again, Harry, I ask you this. Who's the man was ever made any better by a guzzle at the hard stuff? Oh my God, Harry, but Victor's the most melancholy man I've ever met! And mean with it."

"I've certainly seen Vic when he's had things on his mind."

"Did he say anything about me?"

"He thinks very highly of you." Harry wondered why he was lying. He wondered too, if MacQueen had really met Nairn, drink taken, in the street, or if, as Nairn claimed, MacQueen had rung Nairn's doorbell.

"The man's a liar if he gives you that impression. I've been in Victor's house, and there he was, sipping a glass of decent whisky" – Harry Boyle smiled, interested – "and in the course of an hour, an hour," he repeated, with disbelief and raising his voice, "not so much as an offer of a drink. Not even a small one from the same bottle as he had by his elbow. It's as if there's but the one glass in the Nairns' house. And I daresay he keeps his teeth in it at night. Mean. *Mean*. A selfish man." He stared at the pavement, shaking his head in anger at Nairn's inadequate hospitality. "But he always pours another one, for himself."

"Drink taken, you say?"

"Drink taken," MacQueen confirmed. "As a matter of fact," he said sadly, "I've an appointment with the doctor in half an hour. Nasal polyps. Or that's my diagnosis." He offered a view of his nostrils in the light of the Co-op's display windows. "And I'm just generally run down. Otherwise I'm OK. But how are chaps like us to know that? If you ask me, we're very much in the hands of the medical profession, Harry. How about you?" he asked without conviction, looking at his watch.

"Health's fine," said Harry. "Only problem is, I'm broke, as you can well imagine."

"Times are hard." MacQueen looked as if he found other people's problems distasteful. "It's the same all over."

When Harry Boyle got home, he found his wife putting her coat on. She had a cleaning job in the High School and worked from five until seven-thirty. Harry kissed her and pulled her collar up while the dog trotted into the living room, dragging its leash.

"That was some walk," Vera said. "Is anything wrong?"

"Vic Nairn," said Harry, "and then Bob MacQueen. And I had to talk to them. First one," he said, amused at his own anger, "and then the other."

"That'll teach you to walk around the town without looking where you're going."

They could hear their son, Alan, fussing the dog with dog-chat in the living room.

"Leave Sadie's dinner in the oven," Vera said. "And this time, remember to turn it down when you've taken yours out."

It registered on Harry that in the time he had been on his walk, Vera had cooked the dinner. "What's Sadie doing this time that she has to be so late?"

"She told you this morning."

"Did she?"

"She's rehearsing in the school play. She'll be in shortly after six," she said, kissing him before she went out.

For the past year, the Boyles' son had been behaving with high-spirited secrecy. He was fifteen and looked twenty. The

Boyles expected his adolescence to take disturbing contemporary forms, but they were surprised when these came as a jaunty disregard of what they had brought Alan up to believe were the family's conventions. Harry couldn't make up his mind whether to be amused or concerned, silent or censorious. "You were the same at that age," Vera had told him. "So let him get on with it."

"I was not."

"I remember you," she said, "in winkle-picker shoes and singing a daft song about lollipops on the bus."

"Me?"

For anyone other than a few friends and a handful of sinister heroes and heroines with mauve hair, neon complexions, and black leather waistcoats with silver studs, Alan exercised a ruthless contempt. "Walkies? Walkies?" he chirped at the dog, which replied with small barks.

"Y've no intention of taking it a walk," Harry said.

"Walkies? Walkies?"

"Y' *never* take it a walk!"

"It's my dog." He fondled the dog roughly by its neck. "Who's my dog? You're my dog. Aren't you? Walkies?"

"I take it y'know Vic Nairn's son. Alec. That's right, isn't it? Alec? What's Alec Nairn like at school?"

"Walkies?"

"It's got a screw loose. It's been walked stupid. Alec Nairn," he chivvied. "I know he's more Sadie's age, but do y' know him?"

"Walkies? Walkies?"

"I've a problem, son," Harry said. "Whether to throw you across the room, or that mutt. Alec Nairn! What's he like?"

"Alec Nairn's a zombie."

"An' Gerald MacQueen? Do y' know *him*? The plumber's boy – do y' know him?"

"Walkies?" Alan sang, the dog's front paws on his lap, its tail wagging frantically.

His father rose from his chair, lifted the dog, crossed the room, opened the door, and placed the terrier in the hall. He closed the door and sat down again. Alan stared at him with mock admiration for his decisively paternal action. "Gerald MacQueen," Harry reminded him.

"His old man found him down a drain. It's well known. Don't tell me they're running after my sister. I couldn't *stand* it!" He shuddered facetiously and clenched his fists. "Eat," he said. "I've got to eat. I've got to take my mind off it." He walked away. "Walkies? Walkies?" Harry heard him say in the hall as the dog barked.

It crossed Harry's mind that the sons of Nairn and MacQueen were probably well-behaved, neat, short-haired, and studious. Alan was short-haired but wore an earring. He gave no impression of being studious, but his marks were a lot higher than his attitude led his parents to expect.

Harry filled his plate and sat at his place at the kitchen table. "What's on tonight?"

"What day is it?"

"Tuesday."

"Tuesday night," said Alan, "is bondage night."

Harry was not entirely sure what the word meant, but he had a good idea. "Whatever bondage is, you eat that up, because this family can't afford to leave food on the plates."

Alan pushed his half-finished dinner across the table.

"God bless us," said Harry, exasperated. "You know more about the world than I do. Don't y'? Watch it, son. You watch your step. That's all I can say."

Alan walked the kitchen with exaggeratedly careful movements, watching his step.

"I'll give y' a month. An' if y' don't show signs of treatin' your mother an' me to a bit of respect, then you're for the high jump."

"The high jump? I'm good at the high jump."

"What I mean, son, is that if I don't see improvements in you along the lines I've mentioned, I'll put your face in." Alan leaned on the sink, watching his father eat. Harry banged the table with his fist. Alan jumped. "Just testin' your nerve, son. Face in. Got that?"

Sadie was later than Vera had said. As she ate her dinner, Harry asked, "Are you sure this playacting isn't keepin' y' off your studies, girl?" He knew in advance that Sadie would treat his concern as that of a man who left school at fifteen and who had an overstated interest in his daughter's opportunities as a compensation for those he had never had, or had turned down.

"It's Shakespeare. It *is* my studies. *Twelfth Night*", she said, "is on the syllabus."

Harry pointed to the clock on the wall. "Then what about the hour y' spend sittin' in that café?"

"Do you honestly think that I'm the sort of person who'd waste her time failing exams, when I know how much depends on passing them? Give me credit, Dad. A woman has to show a lot more initiative than a man to get on in this country. The cards are loaded against her."

"Dice," said Harry. "Dice can be loaded, but not cards. Cheats *mark* cards. They don't 'load' them."

"A woman has to be more competent, more qualified than a man, just to get the same job. I know how hard I have to work."

"Cards aren't loaded. *Dice*."

"Thanks for the useful information, Dad, but being a topless croupier just doesn't figure in my plans."

"I don't know what to think. I've a daughter who's into women's rights before she's even left school, and a boy who's into bondage. I'm *mesmerized*."

"Bondage? Is that what he says?"

"Tuesday night", said Harry, "is your brother's bondage night."

"He doesn't know what it is."

"Do you know what it is?"

"Of course."

"Well, sure, of course. You're seventeen, an' this is 1981, so of course y' know. Mind you, I haven't paid much attention to it myself, an' if your mother's given it a thought, then she's kept it quiet, thank God, but you know, an' Alan knows, or Alan says he knows . . . That's fine. *Twelfth Night*'s a Shakespeare? Should I read it before we come and watch you act in it? Assumin', that is, we can afford the tickets. Who do y' play?"

"I play Viola. But most of the time I'm Cesario. And he's a man. If you see what I mean."

"I think I'd better read it."

Several days a week, after lunch, Harry and Vera Boyle spent an hour in bed. To begin with, it seemed an extraordinary thing to do, as if, were they discovered, it might bring the unemployed into disrepute.

"I suppose," Vera said, "that this is what rich people do in the afternoon. I could get used to it."

"I'm getting used to it already." Harry did more housework than he had been brought up to believe was good for a man's dignity. "How much would it cost," he asked Vera, "to have these curtains dry-cleaned?"

"I don't think I like what's happening to you. Last week you washed the kitchen floor, behind my back. And now you're talking about curtains."

A few days later: "Have we any carpet shampoo in the house, Vera? I don't see it in the cupboard."

"Have you spilled something?"

"No. But look at it. It's a good few shades darker than when we bought it."

Carpet shampoo materialized, as Vera took advantage of Harry's new housewifery, or husbandry.

"I think it's getting to you," Vera said.

"What is?"

"Unemployment is. And time is, too."

"You don't hear me talk about unemployment. I just don't get roused by the subject. I've got plenty of time."

"You were certainly angry enough the night you came home with that redundancy notice."

"Sure, I was livid. But right now I'm into carpets and curtains. I'm a home boy. If they can keep me on the breadline, plus some, I'll be happy enough and so will you."

"Guess who's your 'plus some'."

"What?"

"Me." Vera smiled.

As Harry came out of the public park, idling while the dog sniffed the length of the open gate, he saw Vic Nairn leave the swimming baths on the other side of the road. An attendant came half-way down the steps with Nairn, in the posture of a man asking a distressed person if he was sure he would be all right. Curious at the sight of Nairn with a rolled towel under his arm, Harry forgot to hide. Nairn saw him and waved with a limp stroke of his arm, waiting on the pavement for Harry to cross the street.

"I'd no idea you were a baths-goer," Harry said.

"According to the doctor, I ought to take more exercise. I told him I didn't think it would help my condition. I've seen the day, Harry, when I could manage thirty lengths of the pool and then go for a long run. Remember, when we were boys, how I used to be such a good swimmer?"

Harry could not find these recollections in his mental album of disagreeable episodes involving Nairn as man and boy. "A powerful swimmer, if I remember correctly, Vic."

"God, that'll teach me." Nairn sighed, dolefully resigned to his physical deterioration. "A length and a half, Harry, and I sank like the Royal Oak. Oh, it was a near thing, Harry. I've been at death's door before now, as you well know, but that's the first time I've seen the doorman. And I know what you're thinking. Why's a hardworking man like me to be seen coming out the baths on a Friday afternoon? I'm on short time. Me, on short time!"

"I'm very sorry to hear that, Vic." Harry worried at his own sincerity.

"Twenty-four years I've given that company. They'll be closing," said Nairn, sonorous with industrial gloom. "I give them three months at the very most. I don't know what I'll do. And there's the humiliation coming, the affront of it all, of having to sign on for the dole, for the unemployment benefit!"

"You'll get used to it," Harry said encouragingly.

"Do you have to stand in a queue, with other men? What I mean is," he whispered, "is it possible – I mean, is there a time when they're not busy? You'll know this, Harry. Can I pop in," he asked furtively, holding Harry by the elbow, "without having to stand in a queue?"

"They'll give you a time, Vic," Harry said.

"We'll not see the likes of Bob MacQueen in a dole queue," said Nairn, his lips smacking with vindictiveness.

"If he goes bust," said Harry, "it's the end of the world. MacQueen's self-employed. He isn't entitled to unemployment benefit."

"He'll have made provisions," said Nairn. "But even so,

here's hoping," he said, his eyes widening, "that the bottom falls out of the plumbing trade."

"I wouldn't go that far," said Harry, jerking the dog on its leash, angry with himself for having given so much as a hint of complicity in Nairn's bad-mindedness. "No, y' wouldn't say a thing like that if you'd been unemployed for as long as I have."

"Oh, don't say that, Harry. I'll find a job. I'll *look* for one."

"I looked as well, y' know."

"I didn't mean it like that, Harry."

"It's new to you, Vic. But you'll find out." He was pleased at having bad tidings of his own to pass on, but checked himself from rubbing them in.

"It's the indignity of it!"

"Forget that," said Harry. "Believe me, it'll pass. Think of all the time you'll have to spend with Mrs Nairn."

"Oh God, no."

"Must make tracks, Vic. Big night out. Sadie's got the star part in *Twelfth Night*."

"My boy Alec's more or less masterminding that!" Nairn's anxious mood changed to one of enthusiastic pride.

"He is?" Pained by this news, Harry persevered in making his escape. "Must go. See y' soon, Vic."

"I'll see you tonight!" Nairn shouted after him, the near-drowning, short time, and threat of no time banished.

In his suit, his white shirt, his best tie, and his best shoes dotingly polished, Harry joined Alan in the living room. He studied his languorous son. "Shakespeare was never up my street, either. But y' could've made the effort. It's your sister I'm going to see, no' Shakespeare. In fact, she plays a man, Cesario, as well as Viola. Same person, really – Viola pretends, y' see, an' dresses up as a man. I would've thought *that* was right up your street. An' look at the trouble your mother's gone to. She's taken her togs in a bag, and she's changing at the school, after three hours' hard work on her knees scrubbin' floors." Harry started temperately and ended up losing his patience. "What's on tonight, then? An' before y' ask, it's Friday."

"I'm in love," Alan said cynically. "I'm staying in to wash my hair, and pine."

During the first interval, after Act II, Harry and Vera stood together drinking coffee from plastic cups in the corridor outside the school's theatre. They smiled at nearby couples. "Did you scrub this?" Harry asked her.

"We don't scrub it. It's parquet," she said. "We do it with a mechanical polisher."

"Who taught Sadie to speak like that? She sounded . . . well, she sounded English."

"That's what I've been wondering."

"What did you think?"

"I think she's terrific."

"But dressed up as a man, wearing a man's clothes – it gave me the fright of my life, love."

"Don't drip coffee," Vera chided, "on my parquet."

"We'll have to keep an eye out," said Bob MacQueen, joining them, accompanied by his wife. "I caught a view there of Victor Nairn."

"What did you think of Gerald, Mrs Boyle?" asked Mrs MacQueen, overdressed, large, and proud. "Malvolio," she said. "Of course, we won't get the best of Malvolio until a little later. Awfully funny, isn't he?"

"Oh, Malvolio! Harry, Gerald's playing Malvolio," Vera said, with a nudge, as if this were good news.

"What's worrying me," said MacQueen, anxiously looking round in case Vic Nairn had spotted them in the crowd, "is that this fairy-tale stuff could go to Gerald's head. Not to mention how much this is costing the ratepayers. Harry, these costumes alone . . . Oh God, the sight of my own son dressed up like an idiot," MacQueen said, in agony, "gives me a *pain*."

"It's a comedy," said Vera.

"I'm not laughing," said MacQueen. "Even if this is Shakespeare, it's just a frill, an extra, and in days like these – well, I don't have to tell you, Harry."

"Business not too good, Bob?" Harry asked, while their wives attempted to submerge their pride in seriousness.

"Business, Harry, is downright awful. I could do with a real cold snap. I need burst pipes. Another mild winter and I don't know what I'll do. And who can afford to install

68

central heating these days? And these nasal polyps? The doctor had the cheek to say I must have broken my nose at some time. Now, if a man had broken his nose, he'd know about it. Wouldn't he? I ask you, Harry . . . " They went into the theatre as the second bell rang and schoolgirls ushered the audience to its seats. "There's something up these nostrils of mine, Harry. I just know it." Harry closed his eyes. He had more than a fair of notion of what, or who, was getting up his own nose. "Any pains yourself, Harry?"

"Not a pain exactly," Harry said. "More a sort of a dull ache, at the back of my neck."

Once seated, Vera said, "Not a word about Sadie. It was Gerald, Gerald, Gerald. And our Sadie has the best part. She's marvellous. But not so much as a mention."

"Oh, no," said Harry, "he's seen us." He returned a wave to Vic Nairn, convinced he would be denied the chance of avoiding him later. "Who's his boy playing? Belch? Aguecheek?"

"'Assistant Stage Manager'," Vera read from the programme, as the lights were dimmed too quickly and then came up again.

In this fresh burst of light, Harry took the programme. "That figures. He's in charge of the lighting." He waved again at the Nairns, this time in a better frame of mind.

Backstage noises were audible, until an urgent voice hushed them. The lights dimmed and then came up again. The curtain rose a few feet – enough to show Viola's legs and the spangled tights of Feste the Clown. Then it dropped like a gesture of irritation. The audience mumbled with polite concern. Older schoolboys stamped their feet. Several hearties let off piercing whistles.

"It's such a pity," said the woman sitting on Harry's left. "They've been doing *awfully* well up to now."

Vera leaned over and said good evening to the couple.

"Our son," said the husband, "is Orsino, the Duke of Illyria."

"Our daughter," said Vera, "is Viola. And Cesario."

"How lovely! They'll be getting married, you know," said the woman they had never seen before.

"Not at this rate they won't be," said Harry.

"What's happening? Have you any idea why it's being

delayed like this?" asked the woman.

"I've a strong suspicion," said Harry, "that the assistant stage manager is a bit like his father."

Lights dimmed, the curtain rose. "Save thee, friend, and thy music," Viola greeted the Clown. "Dost thou live by thy tabor?"

"No, sir," said Feste, sitting on his drum, "I live by the church."

"Our daughter," Harry said to Vera, "is an absolute knockout. She's got a future in this racket."

Andy Dunlop and Gub MacCluskey walked along Sidmouth Street a few minutes after half-past five. "Who the hell was this Sidmouth? Any idea?"

Gub MacCluskey persevered with his ritual of tobacco, paper and fingers. He looked meditative, like a vet tending a small mammal. "It's a place. Sidmouth's the name of a place," he said, stretching the dark tobacco, "down south."

"Now y' mention it . . . It rings a bell. But how come we're lumbered wi' it an' all then?"

"Don't give us that patter. How many streets are there in this town? Any idea? Thousands, that's what. An' it's no' all that big a country, is it? So it stands to reason, Andy."

"Stands to what reason?" asked Andy Dunlop.

"There aren't enough names in Scotland to go round. Places – fair enough, names galore. Streets – no way, Andy. The planners've just got to look elsewhere."

"I'll look that name up in the library." Despite the bell that had rung a moment before, he was no longer convinced. "Mind you, I'll admit it doesn't sound Scottish."

"Neither does Glasgow. It's only because y' know it is that y' *believe* it is."

"I'm sure that's no' a wireless," said Andy Dunlop. They listened. Their eyes roved from one storey of the tenement to the next.

"Benny Craig," said Gub MacCluskey, snapping his fingers. "That'll be who it is. The boy plays the clarinet."

"Davie Craig's boy?"

"Real serious boy, accordin' to Davie. If y' ask me, Davie's worried about that boy."

Staring up, with their faces screwed into pained expressions, they listened while a flock of starlings swept down on a ledge.

"What the hell kind of music *is* that?"

On the fourth floor, in a bedroom he shared with his two

younger brothers, Ted Craig was practising with the devotion of a saint.

"Oh, I get it. Benny *Goodman!*"

"Play it, Benny!" Gub MacCluskey shouted through cupped hands held close to his mouth.

Ted Craig was preparing for an audition. His father still refused to believe he could force an entry on the Glasgow School of Music on the strength of a written test, an interview and a sample of his playing. "Y' haven't the qualifications, son. Y'll have to face up to the fact an' just accept it as a *hobby.*"

"It's no' easy to tap y'r feet to *that*," said Andy Dunlop, whose right shoe was searching the pavement for a beat, smudging a heart drawn in chalk which advertised that two sets of initials were in love with each other.

"Aw, give over!" Gub MacCluskey shouted to the fourth-floor window. No one that high up could hear him. Ted was immersed in Mozart's *Clarinet Concerto*, the part where the clarinet enters for the first time and which – in case you've forgotten it – goes like this:

Ted Craig's mother opened the bedroom door. Television noises came in, and the sound of Ted's playing went out and was enough to make his brothers yell as if they were seriously pained. His eyes turned from his music which was propped against a pile of books on a sideboard. His fingers continued to play the next few bars from memory before he stopped. "A wee cup of tea, son?"

"How can I play this an' drink tea at the same time?"

"Y'r mouth'll get all dry playin' for as long as that."

Ted's father leaned from his armchair by the door until his head was visible. Hearing him clear his throat, Mrs Craig moved to one side. "You wet y'r whistle, son. I've told y', take it easy. If you've a big test comin', then keep somethin' in reserve."

Considerate, peace-making, Mrs Craig closed the door softly behind her and sat down again. "Can y' not turn that thing down a bit?" she said, knowing no one was likely to make a move towards the switch.

Once inside The Wheatsheaf, Gub MacCluskey and Andy Dunlop settled on their elbows before the bar. A man came over to them from the shadows. "Hear y'r all on strike boys," he said.

"Strike? No' us," they said to the small, middle-aged man.

"Oh . . . Oh, well, hell of a sorry, lads." The man backed off. "Awfully sorry. Sorry, boys." Timid confusion made his repeated statements of being sorry sound like condolences. "Hell of a sorry, lads . . . "

"Y' tell him y'r no' on strike, an' he apologizes? What's this world comin' to?" said Gub to Andy.

After a few words to some men who were sitting at a table in the darkness of the bar-room, the small man came back.

"They three there, *they* work at Passmore's, an' *they* say they're *definitely* on strike. *Official*," the man added, belligerently directing a finger several times at no one.

"Aye, sure, that's a fact."

"So?"

"So what? We work at MacCallum's."

"Oh . . . Oh, I *see*."

"Aye."

"Hell of a sorry to've inconvenienced you men in that way." He backed off again. "Oh, God, aye, hell of a sorry."

The man returned to the table in the shadows.

"Who he?" Andy Dunlop asked the barman.

"Him? Everybody calls 'im the Union Man."

"Union Man? Y' mean . . .? Y' mean, *he's* a union *organizer*?"

Touching the side of his head with a finger, the barman said, "He wanted to be. Years ago, mind you. The man's no' aw there. He's a One Man Mental Workers' Resistance Movement."

Ted's father came in and sat on the edge of a bed. He motioned for Ted to keep playing. He was now working on the climactically arpeggiated ending of the first movement.

"Very good, son. It sounds a bit on the hard side."

"It's finger-music. It's aw below the fingers."

"Y'r comin' on, I'll say that. An' y'll no' have long to wait before y' find out what's what either. Y' got the wind up?"

"I don't fancy no' passin' it, if that's what y' mean."

"It wouldn't be the end o' the world, son. Quantity surveying's no' a bad line to fall back on."

"For somebody who wants to play this thing for a livin', it's about as bad as y' can get."

"Where you get y'r musical talent from'll always be a mystery to me. I canny even sing. Y'r mother's *never* been able to carry a tune."

"I've met that one before, Dad – canny be any good, his father canny even sing."

"Don't mind it too much when y'r playin' that man Mozart there. It's when y'r doin' these . . . *scales*. Jesus, son, it's like draggin' y'r teeth down a sheet o' sandpaper. Aye, well . . . I'm right behind y' now, Ted."

"What was it," said Ted, moved but unable to show it, "just a matter of time?"

"Not my time." His father looked at him. "It's the time *you've* spent playin' that thing. You know me, I'm useless at serious conversations." An embarrassed silence grew between them. "Just you play that, son. That's all. If you want to play that, then I take y'r point. You stick in. Wire in, son."

"Thanks, Dad," Ted said. "It'll make a difference, knowin' you don't think I'm wastin' time . . . "

"Play us that bit again," Davie Craig said, sitting back on the bed. "I'd like to hear that bit properly."

"What bit?"

"The bit y' were playin' when I came in. That bit wi' all these notes in it."

"Y' know," said Gub MacCluskey, putting his glass down, "I'm in two minds if I'm right about Sidmouth bein' a place down south. You've confused me."

"It rings a bell, I'm tellin' y'. Right down, right down south somewhere. I think I saw somethin' about that place the year we were in Torquay."

"Torquay?"

"Aye, an' great digs there . . . "

"Sidmouth?" interrupted the Union Man, who was paying for a half-pint in coppers and doling them out one at a time into the barman's hand, knowing he didn't have enough, and knowing that the barman knew.

"Aye, Sidmouth," said Andy Dunlop, turning away from the stranger.

"Right bad man was Sidmouth," said the Union Man.

"It's a *place*. It's a *place*, down south." Gub MacCluskey made it clear he had had about enough of the Union Man.

"A big politico, a long time back . . . One o' the biggest reactionaries ever to cast a shadow on the workin'-man's movement." Each fatalistic emphasis added to Gub Mac-Cluskey's increasing interest. "An' *that* was Sidmouth."

"Never knew anybody catch 'im out on matters of historical importance," said the barman. He rattled his handful of coppers. "Aye, an' another three pence, you."

"Are you sure about this?" asked Andy Dunlop.

"Sure I'm sure," said the small man.

As his price for finding out more, Andy Dunlop took three pence from the pile of coins beside his glass and gave them to the barman. "Awful good of you," said the Union Man, excessively polite. "An' I'm awfully sorry to've intruded on y'r conversation like that, boys."

"We're no' finished wi' you yet," said Gub MacCluskey, catching the Union Man by the coat. "You tell us what y' know about this Sidmouth."

"Way back, in eighteen-twenty or eighteen-whatever-it-was . . . Strike isny the word for it. More like a rebellion. Soldiers in the streets. My mind's no' what it was, boys. I can't remember the way I used to."

"An' this Sidmouth was one o' the swine that sent the troops in?"

"There was some poor radical-man hung, drawn, an' quartered because o' him. Dragged through the streets," said the Union Man, "on a cart, an' then hung an' cut up, in public. Down there, I'm tellin' y', in the Candleriggs."

He sidled away on his shuffling, short footsteps, looking after his half-pint which he held before him like a lamp.

"Don't know about you, but I'm writin' to the Lord Provost. Either they change the name o' that street or I'm takin' up terrorism."

"Take it easy," said Gub MacCluskey. "They're knockin' it down in six months anyway."

"Oh hello, Davie," said Andy Dunlop with more familiarity than Ted's father thought was called for. "We were just talkin' about y'r boy."

"Oh aye, which one?"

"Benny. We heard 'im earlier the night."

"Benny? I don't have a boy called 'Benny'."

"Oh."

"If it's Edward you mean," said Davie Craig, "then you call him that."

"Edward?"

"That's 'is name."

"Aye," said Gub MacCluskey. "Edward seems to be doin' well."

"I hear y'r on strike up at Passmore's," said Davie Craig.

"Och, no' again. We work at *MacCallum's*."

"Oh, sorry, boys."

"An' don't say that either. That's what *he* says."

"Who?" Davie Craig asked, following a nod towards where a small man sat hidden behind an opened second-hand newspaper.

"The Union Man."

"Pour soul," said Davie Craig. "He went on strike once too often."

Davie supped his beer. He began humming a tune. Gub MacCluskey and Andy Dunlop watched and listened. "The Mozart *Clarinet Concerto*," Davie explained. "Great wee tune, eh? I used to think that stuff was *rubbish*."

"*That's* what we heard 'im play," said Gub MacCluskey, snapping his fingers. He hummed the tune. "It's been on my mind, that." He hummed the tune and drummed his fingers on the wet bar. The Union Man lowered his paper to have a quick look at these three men who were humming the opening bars of the clarinet's solo in the first movement of Mozart's *Clarinet Concerto*.

"Oh, there's some lovely music been written," said Davie Craig. "*Lovely*. An' I haven't so much as bought my own boy a lesson. I didn't understand, y'see. But it's a great tune. It's a *great* tune. One of the all-time great melodies in my opinion."

Andy Dunlop and Gub MacCluskey nodded in agreement. Davie began humming the tune again. He was imagining his

76

son sitting by the open bedroom window as his brothers slept, listening to Mozart's *Clarinet Concerto* rise from the city. His two companions joined in. They made gestures with their hands in time to the music. The Union Man looked over his newspaper again. "Oh, but it's a great tune," said Davie Craig. "An' the Slow Movement – the Slow Movement's *magic*." Davie closed his eyes. "While the Rondo – ah-ha, the Rondo *takes off.*"

"Y' know about Sidmouth?" asked Andy Dunlop.

"Sidmouth?"

"*Lord* Sidmouth."

"Aye, I've heard about Lord Sidmouth. I've lived in that street," said Davie Craig, "all my married life."

"Does . . . eh, I mean, does y'r *boy*, Edward, y'r boy wi' the fancy ideas, does *he* know about Lord Sidmouth?"

"Oh, he knows. He knows all right. In more bloody ways than one. Hey, Union Man?" Davie shouted, to the newspaper that was cautiously lowered. "Do y' want a drink, Union Man?"

BOBBY'S ROOM

Henry Pollock was the only child of only children, and his four grandparents were dead. When he was twelve, in 1954, he and his parents left Glasgow on a motoring holiday. They stayed in a succession of hotels all over the Borders and the southwest of Scotland. At one place, they found that the hotels and guesthouses were full. It was a town Mrs Pollock particularly wanted to visit, and all the rooms were booked up for some local annual event. Mr Pollock was irate. His wife chided him for not having telephoned a reservation in advance, as, she said, she had suggested in the first place.

"We said potluck was part of the charm, did we not?" was Henry's father's riposte. Bickering in the car park lasted almost an hour.

Pollock was a tall man, powerful, proud, and successful; Henry had got used to his obstinate refusals to give in to his wife's complaints or preferences, to which, in the end, he always conformed without seeming to surrender. Harsh words when they fell out were, Henry knew, a prelude to that kind of morning on which he didn't see them until it was nearly noon. If these were mornings when he went to school, then his mother hurriedly threw his breakfast together and kissed him on the ear before running back upstairs in her kimono.

Even in the small space of the car, they managed to ignore Henry, and he knew better than to say anything.

"If you're in such a hurry to find somewhere, then why don't you drive?" his father asked Mrs Pollock.

"You know I can't. Don't be so stupid."

"Then allow me to the judge of when we leave and when we don't. I need petrol, in any case."

"You can't possibly need petrol. You filled up this morning in Dumfries."

Eventually they got under way again, and after a few miles Pollock stopped the car outside a substantial stone-built villa, a house much like their own back in Glasgow; a notice board advertised that it offered accommodations.

"What do you think?" he asked.

"I think it's seen better days, that's what I think," said Mrs Pollock, who was still simmering. Her husband went to see if there were two rooms available, and to investigate what the place was like. "It doesn't even have a drive," she said to Henry. "Where will we put the car?"

"I don't see any cars," Henry said, "so they must have rooms."

"When I want your opinion, I'll ask for it. *Netherbank*," she said, sounding the name of the house as proof of its unsuitability.

Pollock returned a few minutes later. "It's first-rate," he said with genuine enthusiasm, leaning into the car. "The rooms are large and spotlessly clean, very airy and spacious, and no one else is staying there." Breezily, he listed the qualifications Mrs Pollock always insisted were necessary for a night's comfort. "We can have the sitting room to ourselves, if we want it, and you'll find the bathroom highly acceptable. I think we should take it. Irene, it's run by a lovely old couple. You'll adore them."

Netherbank was run by a Mrs Bawden. She was over sixty, silver-haired, round, short, respectable, and as Mrs Pollock said afterwards, very nicely spoken. She took it in her stride when Mrs Pollock asked if she could have a look at what she was offering for dinner. "Normally, I prefer a proper res-taurant. But my husband's very tired after a day's driving."

"Some people ask me for what they call an 'evening meal'," Mrs Bawden said, lifting the lid off a saucepan. "I call it dinner. I've always called it dinner, and I won't change now. Round about here, people call lunch dinner. But I call it luncheon, and I call it luncheon at twelve-thirty. And I call tea tea. I don't know where we'll all end up if we begin to call things by the wrong names." Mrs Pollock couldn't agree more.

They stayed for five nights. Henry knew one of the reasons his parents liked the place so much: Mrs Bawden was very obliging. Before Mrs Pollock could ask, Mrs Bawden offered to keep an eye on Henry if they wanted to go off by themselves for a day, or go to dinner in a hotel restaurant about ten miles away which Mrs Bawden had heard was outstanding for its seafood. "But Mrs Bawden, you'll do yourself out of business," his mother said.

"No, no, I won't. You're on holiday, and it'll be my pleasure to help you enjoy yourselves." Mrs Pollock revelled in being the beneficiary of that sort of consideration. Henry's parents had three days on their own without him, and three evenings at the famous restaurant.

Henry wandered round the hills and farms, and walked the two miles to the sea. He read, and he watched Mr Bawden at work in his garden. The old man was hard of hearing, or said he was, and when Henry tried to talk to him he pointed to an ear, smiled, and went back to his weeding or hoeing.

These were the last days of their holiday. His parents loved it. "I haven't felt so refreshed and well in years!" said Henry's mother as they drove home. "And Mrs Bawden – what a wonderful woman! Her cooking's pre-war! We were lucky to find it. It's the sort of place you could drive right past without giving it so much as a moment's notice." After that, she and her husband looked at each other in the way that made Henry feel he wasn't there. A little later, Mrs Pollock started to sing. She coaxed Henry to join in. When he didn't, she turned round and said, "You'll grow up to be miserable. Why won't you sing, like the rest of us?"

Two years later, there was a week in early June when Henry's father was more thoughtful than usual. After dinner he did a lot of meditative gardening. Tired of that, he sat in the lounge with an open book on his lap. Henry's mother brought him tea or coffee, asked him if he wanted something stronger, or something to eat, and in her busy efforts to leave him alone made a nuisance of herself. It was obvious to Henry that his father was making his mind up about something important. From time to time he saw his parents talk quietly and seriously to each other. They cuddled in the kitchen even more often than usual.

"Why don't I phone her? I kept a note of the number, you know," he heard his mother say one evening.

"Do you think she would?" Pollock asked her. "It's not really what she does."

"Almost three months at her usual rates is probably very good business for her, especially if we add something on for her trouble. I imagine she'll be only too pleased."

"It'd be ideal. But what do we do about the weeks of school he'll have to miss?"

"Darling, I've no intention of being left behind. It's an opportunity to travel I won't let pass by, especially since the offer specifically includes me as well. It's not as if you'll have to fork out for my fare and hotel bills. Some of us were prevented from travelling by the war, you know, not to mention marriage and motherhood."

"If this trip's successful, there will have to be others, as a matter of course. It's a big project. It's not one bridge, it's a network. I don't look forward to going away without you, and I want you to come with me. But the best thing might be to start thinking about boarding school."

"Were Henry younger, I'd say no, naturally. But at his age boarding school is probably a very adventurous proposition. I know it was for Alice Wylie's brother."

Later that evening, Henry heard the telephone being used. He looked down into the hall from the top of the stairs and saw his mother leaning against the opposite wall while his father spoke into the phone. She was smoking, which she did only in company to be polite, or when she was agitated. Then she, too, went over to the phone and began to speak into it. Later, his mother called him to come down to the sitting room.

"Your mother and I have to go to Singapore," his father said. "We'll be gone for most of July and all of August and September. And I'm afraid it just isn't practical to take you with us."

"You remember Mrs Bawden, and Netherbank?" His wife spoke sooner than Pollock would have liked. "We've arranged for you to stay with her."

"What about school?" Henry's tone of voice was meant to suggest that weeks of missed classes could be disastrous.

"Henry, you're the last person I can imagine slipping behind. A few weeks won't be a setback to you."

His mother's way of speaking to him, her confidence in his

maturity and academic excellence, made Henry want to fight back. He felt inclined to be stubborn and obstructive. "There isn't a lot to do at Mrs Bawden's," he said.

"We both think it's ideal."

"We've no choice but to leave you behind." his father said. "We'll be happier, much happier, knowing you're somewhere we can feel easy in our minds about."

Henry looked at his mother, hoping she would understand that he expected her to stay behind with him. She said, "I'll talk to the headmaster on Monday. You can arrange for your teachers to give you a programme of study. You can do it on your own – I'm sure you can. And if you think you can't, you're underrating yourself." He knew enough about her to know that if at his age she had been given a "programme of study" she'd have collapsed in tears.

Instead of making it difficult for them, he accepted it, and resigned himself. He knew why they had chosen Mrs Bawden and Netherbank. They had been happy there, and assumed that he had liked it, too. It was a place and a few days in their lives that meant something in their happiness. He wondered why they could continue to be so ignorant of his feelings. Mrs Bawden was not a complete stranger, but she was the next thing to it – the landlady of a guesthouse, a species his mother usually loathed.

"Don't feel unwanted," his mother said. "It would suit us better, much better, if you could come with us. But it isn't possible, so we have to make the best of it."

When the time came, they drove him to Mrs Bawden's with suitcases, books, tennis racquet, binoculars, and field guides to the birds and wildflowers of the British Isles. Nature study was his mother's idea. "When I get back, I want to find you thoroughly up to the mark in country life," she said. "It's a wonderful opportunity for you. I've always been opposed to townies." He tried to think of what it was she craved so determinedly that it made a trip to Singapore necessary to her.

She wept as she said goodbye. Henry felt like weeping on his own account.

"I know you won't give Mrs Bawden any trouble," she said. It was the wrong thing to have said. Obedient to the point of filial perfection, he had never given anyone the least bit of trouble in his life.

"How long does post take from Singapore?" Mrs Pollock asked her husband.

"Airmail," he said. "Pretty fast."

"Then I'll write at least once a week, and I'll expect you to do the same," she told Henry. With that, she left for the car, dabbing at her eyes with a handkerchief.

"You haven't left me your address in Singapore," Henry said. Pollock had to call for Mrs Bawden to bring a piece of paper for him to write it down on. He was embarrassed, talking about rush, last-minute details, oversights.

Henry had reckoned on eating alone in the dining room, like any other guest, but he ate with the Bawdens in their kitchen. "No aunts, no uncles," said Mr Bawden, as the old couple explored Henry's family. "So no cousins, either. No great loss, if you ask me. A big scatter of kin makes you feel guilty at not keeping in touch, which you can't do, you know, unless you're a man of means and leisure."

"I've second cousins," Henry offered.

"I was closer to two of my second cousins than to any of my first," said Mrs Bawden.

"I've never met them," said Henry.

"Singapore's a long, long journey," she said, pushing a bowl of cauliflower towards him.

"Home-grown," said Mr Bawden. "We haven't eaten a tinned vegetable in twenty years."

As he lay awake in bed, Henry pondered his affection for his parents, and decided it was becoming as distant and routine as his parents' love of him. They were his parents, therefore he loved them; he was their son, therefore they loved him – it was as mathematical as that. Co-operation between them was beginning to thin out, like the darkness in the triangle of dawn now at the top of the curtains. His mother prodded him to be the scholar of his class at school, and was proud of his examination victories; but she nagged him for being too studious and staying in when he should have been outside and complained of his lack of interest in sport. They expected him to be perfect, but they neglected him.

He had a different room from the one he had slept in two years before. It was at the front of the house, under the eaves; from its protruding window he could look at a small wedge of sea and the right-hand tip of an island that could be walked to at low tide over the sands. Darkness turned to a transparent grey, and objects in the room slowly became visible. Shelves in an alcove contained dozens of books of boyish interest – books on ships and the sea, the Empire, foreign countries, warlike history, wildlife, fishing, landmarks in engineering and exploration, most of them heavy and already obsolete. There was a home-made model warship on a chest of drawers. Pictures on the wall did not quite cover the cleaner paint left behind from those that had been taken down. His dressing gown, on the hook behind the door, looked like another person in the room. He imagined that the owner of the books was a long-lost son of the Bawdens, dead, probably, in the war.

"Was my room your son's?" he asked Mr Bawden, who pointed to his ear as Henry began to repeat his question.

"We thought you'd like it better than the rooms we let to the holidaymakers," he said. "Or *she* did. You'll find out," he said, as if excusing himself in advance for any apparent lack of initiative on his part. "Mrs Bawden is the boss round here. She wears the trousers."

"Where is he?"

"I haven't the foggiest. Somewhere or other." He jabbed his rake on the dusty ground. "It's good soil for carrots. And there's no better earth for potatoes."

"Is he dead?"

"Good God, no. What gave you that idea? All that's wrong with Bobby is that he's a bit wayward when it comes to writing letters. What made you think he was dead?"

Henry was embarrassed, and with no way of explaining himself. Mr Bawden shrugged and retreated into his deafness and gardening.

Mrs Bawden was obviously told of Henry's questions in the garden. At dinner she recounted Bobby's travels – his letters from Australia, where he had spent three years, the good job in Hong Kong he'd thrown up on a whim in order to go to Canada. "We're about due a letter from him soon."

"What's that?" her husband asked.

"I said we're about due a letter from Bobby."

"I'll believe it when I see it," said Mr Bawden.

When Henry offered to do Mrs Bawden's shopping, it seemed as if she had been expecting him to ask. She gave him a list, and he pedalled the two miles to the nearest shop on a bicycle that had been Bobby's.

A family of five moved in, and stayed for three nights. They were boisterous, but their liveliness appeared toned down out of respect for someone else's house. Mrs Bawden had that effect on people. Henry kept out of their way. When he came down to say good night, Mr Bawden, alone in the kitchen with a book, directed him to the guests' sitting room. He found Mrs Bawden there with the father and mother of the visiting family.

"And this is Bobby in his uniform," she was saying.

"My, he's a fine-looking young man."

"And here's another one, with some friends of his from the same ship."

"I'm off to bed now," Henry told her.

"Good night, Henry."

He was disconcerted by the sight of Mrs Bawden on the sofa, with a guest on either side of her, showing photographs of her son to people she had never seen before and might never see again. There was an amiable candour in her affectionate disappointment in Bobby, and it jolted Henry, who saw it as a failure of reticence, an openness that compromised her loyalty to her son. Snapshots of her son were being touted to strangers and were symptoms of an unhappiness she was too proud to notice.

"Is it all right if I take a cup of cocoa upstairs with me?" he asked Mr Bawden.

"Help yourself," said the old man. Henry boiled the kettle and opened the cocoa tin. "What is it, through there?" Mr Bawden asked. "Snapshots and airmail letters?"

"What?"

"My wife, what's she doing?"

"She's talking to the guests."

"See any photographs?"

"I think she *is* showing them photographs."

85

The old man went back to his book.

Henry wondered how Mrs Bawden selected the people who were treated to her photograph albums. Perhaps everyone was, and perhaps his parents, two years before, had been shown the same photographs, with the same pride, and had listened to the same reminiscences. He felt sure that the visiting couple would have asked who Henry was, and been told that his parents had gone to Singapore, that his father was a civil engineer, and that they had stayed at Netherbank and thought it an ideal place to board their son while they were away. "You ought to come home, Bobby," he said to the vanished son. "Not only does your mother miss you, but she talks about you to people she hardly knows. Worse, she's probably talking about me."

There was a visitors' book on the hall table. Besides putting down their names and addresses, guests over the years had written their comments in a column where remarks were invited. "We had a wonderful time." "Smashing food!" "Highly recommended!" "Excellent." Henry leafed back to two years earlier. "First-class!" his mother had written, in her bold, clear, self-assured handwriting. It was characteristic of her. Any time they travelled by train, his mother made it clear that they went first-class as a matter of course, and that some people did not – never would, never could.

As soon as the family of five left, Netherbank was full almost every night. His parents had found the house to their taste because they had it to themselves, and they were lucky. People often had to be told that there were no rooms left.

Henry tried to keep away from the guests as much as he could, but it was impossible not to ask Mrs Bawden each morning if there was anything she wanted him to do. "Maybe you don't think it's man's work," she said, "but I could fair do with someone to strip the beds this morning and bring the linen down here for me to launder." As the days went by he found himself aproned, pulling linen from beds, vacuuming carpets, dusting furniture, cleaning windows and mirrors, polishing the bannister.

"Next time we hear from you," said Mr Bawden, "you'll be

running a hotel. You've taken to it. But don't tell me you like it. Believe me, I know – no one better. She's a hard woman to refuse."

A girl from Lincolnshire, about Henry's age, passed him in the hall and said, "You must be blind. What's that, then, if it isn't carpet fluff? There," and she pointed. Later the same morning, egged on by a friend who was along on holiday with that family, the girl asked him, "Is this your career? Or is it a punishment?"

"Have you been very bad?" the other girl said, giggling.

"Shoo!" Henry waved a duster at them, and they ran away delighted and laughing.

Breakfast was at seven for the Bawdens and Henry, so that they could eat before the rush of holiday families to the dining room. "The Abercrombie children are sleeping three to a bed," said Mrs Bawden. "I told Mr Abercrombie it was the best I could do, and he was only too pleased to accept. The English family are just the same. There'll be eighteen for breakfast. I've never been so busy."

"Why folk go on holidays I'll never know," said Mr Bawden.

"Do you want me to wait on the tables?" Henry offered.

Mr Bawden gave him an uncertain look, and shook his head in a gesture of subdued bewilderment. "Eighteen," he said. "She could never cook and serve at the same time – not for eighteen."

"You ask them what they'd like," said Mrs Bawden, patting his hand appreciatively. "We have fruit juice. We have porridge and packet cereals. This morning we have kippers, and we have eggs, bacon, sausages, and those who want a fried breakfast are to be asked if they want black pudding with it. Some don't like it, others love it. I never need to take a note, but it might be for the best if you were to write down the orders, like a proper waiter. Eggs scrambled, fried, boiled, or poached. Tea or coffee, and toast, jam or marmalade. And if someone high and mighty asks you for kedgeree, look daft and pretend you've never even heard of it."

"Should I get changed?"

"Put on my big white apron and you'll look the part well enough. And don't be nervous. We're not the Ritz," she said.

Mr Bawden slipped out into the garden with his second cup of tea.

Most guests chose to come down at eight-thirty, and within the space of a few minutes the dining room was full. Henry was surprised that they could be so fussy about what to eat.

"Are the sausages fresh?" a man asked.

"I can't see Mrs Bawden serving you a bad sausage, sir."

"What's a black pudding?"

"Black pudding," Henry said, with a hesitant shrug.

"But what's it made of?"

"Hold on." He asked Mrs Bawden what black puddings were made of, and Mr Bawden, rinsing his cup at the sink, raised his eyebrows.

Henry came back from the kitchen. "Blood and lights," he said.

"I'll have two lightly poached eggs. No, wait a minute. Did you say there were scrambled eggs? In that case, I'll have scrambled eggs."

The two girls from Lincolnshire giggled as Henry stood in his apron with his pad and pen poised. The mother ordered them to hurry up. The father looked seriously at Henry, as if he thought he had been up to something.

By ten o'clock, Henry and Mrs Bawden were alone in the kitchen, tired out and hot and sipping tea. "My twenty-of-everything set of breakfast china came in handy," she said. Most of it was stacked beside the sink. "The Lord be thanked, nobody wants lunch. Rooms next, then laundry. I don't know what I'd do without you, Henry. Next year I'll have to get a village girl to come in."

Mr Bawden appeared with the mail.

"It's another letter from your mother!" Mrs Bawden said. She gave it to Henry. "Go on, read it."

His mother's cadences were in every line. They had been here, there, and seen that and other things. They had developed a taste for Chinese and Malayan food, although they'd been a bit suspicious at first.

"Is it so private that you can't read it out to me?" Mrs Bawden asked. Her husband hurried outside with a cup of tea in one hand and his watering can in the other. "Does she say anything about the climate this time?" she said, remembering the first letter. "Have they got over that exhausting journey? I didn't like the sound of the airport at Karachi."

He glanced through the rest of the letter, to make sure his mother hadn't written anything embarrassing, thinking that it was only to be expected that an old woman who showed her snapshots to all and sundry would take it for granted that a letter should be shared. He read out his mother's account of the strange food, the deliciousness of which his parents had come round to accepting, and the sightseeing. "'Daddy's had to fly up to Penang for a couple of days, so I've been left on my own. Everyone's extremely kind, and I've been playing a very great deal of bridge but as yet no mah-jong, thank goodness. We've been out for dinner every night since we arrived, and I shall be quite plump when I see you next. We look forward to a quiet evening by ourselves. Our bungalow is bijou but not quite as colonial as I would have liked. I'm not very geographical, as you know, and I wasn't quite sure where Singapore was, but I know now, Henry, and I don't mind telling you that it's ABSOLUTELY TROPICAL. It was so nice of you to press a flower in your letter. It made me feel quite homesick.'"

"What a nice young man you are for doing a thing like that," said Mrs Bawden. She patted his hand. "I knew it," she said. "I knew it'd be hot there."

A girl from an Edinburgh family asked Henry if he played tennis. He said he did. She asked if there was a court. He told her where the nearest one was, two miles away in the village.

"I don't have anyone to play with," she said. She didn't sound as if she wanted particularly to play with Henry.

Her mother appeared at the door of the sitting room. "Are you coming with us, or are you staying behind?" The woman's voice stated these options firmly, and Henry recognized the predicaments of both girl and parents.

Mrs Bawden came to the sitting-room door.

"Have you asked him?" the woman said to her daughter.

"It's two miles away," the girl said, meaning that the court was too far to be practical.

"We'll drop you off at the court," said her father from inside, through a rustle of newspaper.

"You haven't had proper company for nearly a month," Mrs Bawden said to Henry. "Go and play tennis if you want. I can answer the door and do what needs to be done. I can manage well enough without you."

He ran upstairs, changed, got his racquet and a box of tennis balls. When he came down, the family of three was waiting in the hall, and the front door was open. The breeze disturbed the potpourri in the bowl on the hall table.

"I'm told that your father and mother are in Singapore," said the man when they were in the car. "Very interesting," he said. "Very interesting." Henry had the impression he had been vetted and found to be a suitable companion for the girl.

"What's your name?" he asked her as they strolled to the tennis court.

"Louise," she said.

"I know what it's like. At least yours haven't gone to Singapore."

"I wish they would."

"My mother's forgotten something, and it probably hasn't dawned on her yet. I'll be fifteen in a couple of weeks and she won't be here."

"It isn't much of a tennis court," Louise said.

She got bored and sat down, ignoring Henry's tepid but ironic serves as they bounced close beside her. Looking at her, he thought that there might be two major ways in which only children could turn out: they became either super-obliging, obedient models of courtesy and good behaviour or, like Louise, rebelliously surly and aggrieved. He never allowed his own grievances to show, and doubted if he ever would.

"When did your father say he'd pick us up?"

"He didn't."

"What do you think of Mrs Bawden?"

"She certainly doesn't have any secrets."

"And Mr Bawden?"

"I didn't know there was one. I thought she was a widow."

"No secrets?"

"I feel sorry for Bobby," she said. "I couldn't stand it if my parents talked about me like that."

"She misses him," Henry said charitably, although he was

interested that Louise disapproved of Mrs Bawden's lack of reticence as much as he did.

"I think I'd like to travel," Louise said. "My father says that air travel will grow enormously in the next few years. I would like to be an air hostess."

"It's Bobby's room I've got. I think I'd like him. I imagine myself talking to him. I ask him what he'd do in my circumstances."

"And I suppose you get some sort of mysterious answer," she said sarcastically. "Do they have a gramophone in that house? I haven't heard a single decent record since we came away."

"He doesn't say anything," Henry said. "But I see him winking at me. I don't know what it means. Do you ever try to figure out what your dreams mean?"

"Isn't there somewhere we can get lemonade or something?" she said peevishly. "I'm parched."

"We could buy some in the shop," he said, "but there isn't a café."

"What a dump!"

"I don't think you like being in the country."

"I don't like being with my parents. I'd rather be in the city with my friends. At least there's something to do."

"Is your father coming back for us?"

"I doubt it. I think we're expected to walk."

She was unsympathetic and, Henry decided, stupid. She was also unhappy. It was her unhappiness that made her interesting. Her dislikes, her petulant good looks, her tone of voice gave the impression she was festering on the edge of a bitter family insurrection. He wondered what his father had found appealing in his mother. Louise made him think that his mother might have been like her at that age, twenty years before, in the nineteen-thirties. All that would have been different was that other kinds of music, other friends were being missed.

They walked back slowly. When they reached Netherbank, Louise's father's car was parked outside with several others. Her parents were in the garden with the Bawdens. The clear light peculiar to Galloway seeped out of the hill and fields and met a great arc of early-evening light rising from the sea. Louise's parents were holding hands. Henry thought that if his parents had been there, too, he would have experienced a moment in which the significance of how people exist to each other was clear and unmistakable. People who mattered less clouded the issue. He pressed Louise's hand, but she pulled it away.

At mid-morning the following day, Louise's father said to Henry, "Do you keep an address book? If you don't then you should. Everyone ought to. Say goodbye, you two," he said, looking at Louise. Henry felt that Louise had given a glowing report of him to her parents, even though, in his company, she had been standoffish, pert, and sardonic. "You should exchange addresses and keep in touch," her father added. He was strangely open and affable.

Louise produced her address book, and Henry dictated his address to her.

"I think that's very nice," said Mrs Bawden. "I think it's so nice," she said to Louise's mother, "that young people should exchange addresses and keep in touch."

Mr Bawden came in by the front door, surprised to find guests still in the house that late in the morning. He could hardly turn round and go out again and found himself in the company.

"They're exchanging addresses. Isn't that nice, John?" his wife said.

Mr Bawden smiled at his wife, with whose obsessive and candid garrulity he was very tenderly and very gently browned off.

"Write letters," she urged Louise. "Write letters and use the phone only when you have to. Letters are *much* nicer. You can keep letters, but you can't keep phone calls. Have you taken a note of Louise's address?" she asked Henry.

"My book's upstairs. I'll take it from the visitors' book."

As Mrs Bawden went out of the front door with Louise's parents, Henry followed with Louise. "We don't have to write," he said.

"I'm not good at letters. If you write first, you'll have a wait for an answer."

"I don't think I'll ever forget you," he said, "but I don't know if you'd understand why." She looked at him, and laughed quietly, but she was complimented by a surprising remark that sounded serious and mature. Her wave from the departing car was curious and concerned.

Henry waved back, and then went upstairs to strip those beds that needed to be freshly made for the arrival of new guests in the late afternoon and early evening. He suspected that a time would come when his parents would regret the three months in which they had hived him off to the Bawdens. He thought about the crisis that his awakening independence would cause in their lives; still he doubted if when it arrived they would be able to trace it back to his weeks in that safe, homely, and respectable house, or to that quaint old couple who lived in daily expectation of a letter from their son Bobby, in whose room Henry slept.

THE BAGPIPING PEOPLE

Two or three mornings a week, in summer, a tinker called Robertson bagpiped the Gilchrist family from sleep half an hour before the time set on its alarm clocks. He played on the hoof, walking along the edge of a narrow plantation of birch trees.

"I thought you liked bagpipes," said Jim Gilchrist, teasing his father's short temper at the breakfast table. "Any time there's a pipe band on the wireless, you always have it turned up. You're the man who wants to go to the Edinburgh Tattoo. Military nostalgia," he said, with a lighthearted, sneering conclusiveness. "It's like a plague in this country. I don't suppose you noticed, but last winter there seemed more pipe bands on the wireless than usual. Suez."

"Is that a fact?" Mr Gilchrist replied.

"No different," said Jim, "from these countries you read about where the radio stations pump out military music while the rebels and the government troops fight it out on the streets. Hungary," he said, the way he had said "Suez" a moment before.

"I worry about your mind," said his father, before tasting his first spoonful of porridge. "Aw, Sadie! You haven't salted it! Again," he said wearily, plopping his spoon into his plate.

"I did salt it," his wife said, with her back to them as she turned the frying bacon and eggs with a fish server. Almost to herself, she added, "I salted it the same as I always salt it."

Sam Gilchrist's porridge never seemed salty enough on these mornings when Robertson's piping woke him up at six. While he sprinkled extra salt on his porridge, his son measured a spoonful of sugar and then, when he knew his father was watching him, sifted it over his porridge.

"Men," Mr Gilchrist said, with a jab of his spoon, "don't put sugar on their porridge."

"I don't see why not," Jim said. "You put jam on your cheese."

"When the tinker's pipes make him so bad-tempered," Mrs

Gilchrist said, "you'd think he'd take the trouble to ask the man to play half an hour later, when he's up anyway. Would that be unreasonable?"

"Perfectly reasonable," said Jim.

His father left the table and opened both kitchen windows. Robertson's piping was too far away to be loud, but there was no doubting it was there.

"They're tinkers," said Sadie Gilchrist. "They're used to taking a telling. Used to it," she emphasized, "week in, week out. It's not as if your father would be asking him never to play within our hearing. Half an hour. What's half an hour in a busy day?"

"I don't mind when or where he plays," said Gilchrist.

"He says he doesn't mind." She sighed with disbelief. "You minded, loudly, at six this morning! He says he doesn't mind! You should've heard him."

The Robertsons and other tinker families lived in an untidy encampment two fields away from the Gilchrists' house. Tarpaulins were stretched over arched metal supports to form tents. It looked like a village of nomadic tribesmen. They possessed a small, open-backed lorry, three horse-drawn carts, and a number of ponies that grazed on lane-side grass or in the waste ground between the pillboxes and blast walls of a wartime anti-aircraft gun position.

By nine in the morning, Robertson would take up his station on the tree-darkened minor road that descended to the ferry. All day in summer, he piped up and down the queues of waiting cars. At times, the queues were long and profitable. In bad weather, only a few cars waited in a short, wet line of mechanized patience. Commercial vehicles, whose drivers were working and not on the road for pleasure, gave no money and were a waste of the piper's wind and skill. Robertson wore a kilt, brown jacket, and off-white open-necked shirt, and went sockless in a pair of brown brogues blanched by a lack of polish and too much weather and walking. He was followed by his daughter. She was about seventeen, and she wore the same green dress day after day, and the same patched sweater. The only variation in her clothing was a light scarf she tied under her chin. Red-haired, flushed, sullen, and barefooted for effect, she had the job of rattling the change in her cloth moneybag at the windows of each car. When it rained, father and daughter stood together under the overhang of the trees – never in the wooden shelter for pedestrians and cyclists.

To contend with the summer traffic, the ferry employed an extra hand, and for the last three years this summer job had been Jim Gilchrist's. At each end of the dismal vessel was a metal ramp, raised and lowered on chains, which when dropped on the cobbled gradients that led into the water allowed the vehicles to drive on and off. Superstructure on either side of the craft rose to an upper deck with benches that doubled as life rafts. On fine days most passengers went up on deck. In the middle of the ferry there was room for ten cars, fewer if a bus or a lorry or a furniture removal van got there first. Entire cycling clubs, local pedestrians, ramblers, hitch-hikers all used the ferry, as well as holidaying motorists, and vans and lorries on every conceivable commercial mission. People came from miles around to watch the ferry's clumsy, clanking, humorous crossings, to wonder at its workhorse appearance, its homely, functional looks, its strength, and then to take a round trip.

Ice cream could be bought from Italian vans on either side of the river. Small boys used the ferry for imaginary adventures. The river stank of oil and an unmistakable, non-specific industrial aroma compounded of shipbuilding, engineering, and the city of Glasgow, through which it flowed before reaching there. Often, the ferry waited for freighters to go by. Passengers waved to sailors, and the ships hooted as their wash approached the ferry and waves broke on the cobbled spits, sluicing around the wheels of the cars as they boarded slowly and carefully, and a ferryman ushered them to come on faster.

Ashton, one of the regular conductors, spent much of his time chasing after passengers and asking to see their tickets. He lived in the hope of catching locals from the south bank whom Jim had let on board free of charge. Jim watched Ashton double-checking tickets, and in his turn he kept his eyes open for natives of the north bank whom Ashton's counter-generosity allowed to cross without paying the fare.

"That was my brother you charged, Jim," Ashton said.

"Sorry, Wattie. I'd no idea."

"No idea? He crosses this river twice a day! He even looks like me. If you think you can come it wi' me, then forget it. It's no skin off my nose if your father knows a big wheel in the Navigational Trust," he said, prodding Jim in the chest. "I'm a lifelong socialist. I don't hold wi' this job-getting through friends of friends or who your daddy knows."

"So what? I'm a lifelong socialist myself."

"You? You aren't even weaned yet."

The ferry was pulled across on parallel chains turned on board in engine houses that were open for small boys and their fathers to watch. "Lovely piece of engineering!" "You're doing a fine job there!" men called to the engineer, who felt himself to be the most watched man in Scotland. Each time the vessel left its cobbled, slippery jetties and the tension was taken up on the chains, they whipped out of the water with a dripping shudder. Women hid their faces in their hands with fear that the massive links might snap, and the strange blue-and-white metal box in which they were crossing the river end up drifting at the mercy of the current as helplessly as a biscuit tin.

"Stand back from the chains there!" Ashton's manner had the fulsome pomposity of the ancient trade of ferryman.

"If you had your way, Ashton, you'd ban bridges. Your days are numbered. One day, the twentieth century'll get wise to this contraption."

When he wasn't playing his pipes and Jim walked past, the tinker always had a civil greeting. "And how's the wee boatie?"

Like everyone else, Jim brought sandwiches for lunch, but he was the only one who went ashore to eat them. Jim never saw Robertson or his daughter eat anything. They went over the wall up the road from the ferry ramp, and into the park that surrounded a hospital for disabled and blind ex-servicemen. There they lit a fire in the same spot every day, seven days a week, and brewed tea.

"That's a very old-looking set of pipes you play, Mr Robertson." Jim imagined that the girl looked surly because she didn't like his knowing their name. It was known among their own kin and kind, but apart from that it was known only to inquisitive policemen, various inspectors from the County Council, and a few farmers. "How old are they?" Jim asked.

"What would a summer boatie like you know about pipes and pibroch?" said Robertson as he stooped over his fire.

"Nothing," Jim admitted.

"And you don't look as if you want to learn," the tinker said slyly, smiling over his tin mug of tea. "Auld pipes," he said, "play auld tunes."

"I'm one of the few people in this world who hear them at six in the morning," Jim said amiably.

"You've heard me play," said Robertson, "you've heard the best you'll ever hear."

"Would you like a sandwich?" Jim asked father and daughter. "I've got more than I need. My mother thinks there must be two of me." The girl nodded a surprised no and walked away, scattering the dregs of her tea on the ground. Strong tea brewed on an open fire and drunk from tin mugs clutched in hot hands is not to be despised, and Jim hoped that Robertson would offer him some. "I've egg, salmon paste, or dried dates," he told the tinker.

"No palm trees where I come from," said Robertson. He took another drink of tea, with an audible slurp.

"I don't suppose my father's complained to you about your six-in-the-morning rehearsals?"

"Your dad and me get on right fine," said Robertson.

"But you play all day, every day. It must be some strain on the wind. I don't understand why you'd want to play at six in the morning as well."

"The last time I saw your dad, he was telling me how he fair misses it when I'm gone. He gave me a dozen eggs that time, and he promised to have a word wi' the farmer, Irvine, and pave the way for my two boys, helping them to a paid job for a week or two. Which your father did. He's a man whose word's as good as a deed done. They'll no' find it easy to make that man change as the clock changes, for all his prosperity."

Summer was Sam Gilchrist's busiest time of the year. He ran a garage, and the major part of his business lay in the sale and repair of tractors and other agricultural machinery. He was beginning to prosper with the nineteen-fifties and saw better times ahead. He worked hard, and it was after seven by the time he got home. He ate, smoked, read the newspaper, dozed with it on his lap; then he woke up and stretched, yawned, and said, "Right. Bedtime."

"Your father," said Sadie Gilchrist, "is a wonderful conversationalist."

"I hear you gave the tinker a dozen eggs," Jim said. "This is a man who gives handouts to an alarm clock."

"And you're the man who's over-fond of his bed. Pass them a few eggs now and then," said Gilchrist, "and they'll be less inclined to help themselves. I've known men like Robertson go through a hen hut just like that – *psst*," he said, cutting his throat with his forefinger. "And there's your eggs gone, and half your hens as well."

"And then he uses his influence with Sandy Irvine. Jobs," said Jim, "for two tinkers. He's even told Robertson how much he dotes on his bagpiping."

"Don't complain, then," said Sadie Gilchrist, "if he serenades us outside the bedroom window."

"I go a long way back with Robertson. It's not how I'd live, but he has a decent streak, and it suits me to give him a helping hand when I feel like it."

During his lunch-hours, Jim observed the habits of the motorists as Robertson piped and his daughter begged with her jangling moneybag. He saw men and women open their car doors and listen with folklorist attentiveness. In his ferryman's uniform, he felt like a cross between a naval officer and a bus conductor; he noticed them size him up as an object of curiosity. Many people gave the girl a copper coin or two with a smile and good grace. Others wound up their windows and looked away when it came their turn for the tinker's daughter to shake her cloth bag before them. Her look then was sharp and peremptory. Jim saw people begin conversations with their companions when they saw her coming, to give the impression that they were too busy doing something else to notice she was there.

At the busiest times, the queue, the ferry, the riverside had the atmosphere of a fair. Children ran down the line of cars to and from the ice cream vans. Money changed hands for ice cream, lemonade, and bagpiping. The Hospital for Disabled Ex-Servicemen had a small showroom at its park gate in which the patients displayed and sold their wares in basketwork. Coin boxes for donations towards the hospital's work were carried up and down the queue by volunteers. Hills on the north bank rose high enough to stand as a promise of the Highlands, toward which many of the motorists were headed. At other stopping places – ferries, scenic spots, ruins and castles – they would come across more bagpipers, other conscientious daughters urging them to part with a few pennies. They were like a secret population, these bagpiping people.

"Four years back," said Ashton, "there was a piper who took up a pitch on the north shore. He'd no license for it, so the police moved him on, and thank God for that. There were bagpipes there and bagpipes over there, and in the middle of the very river the two wails met, and the racket made your hair stand on end. No kidding," he said. "It made my teeth itch. I hate bagpipes. They remind me of the Army."

"Somehow," Jim said, "I thought you were in the Navy."

"Funnyman, aren't you?"

"It's the way you talk, Ashton. 'Port' this, 'starboard' that, 'amidships' – "

"I've been watching you, and I've noticed. Don't think there's a lot goes on here that Wattie Ashton doesn't see. I've seen you, sitting on that wall, and I've seen the way you look at that tinker's daughter." Ashton nodded, approving of his own moral malevolence. "Call yourself educated?"

Over and back again, over and back again – north bank, south bank, north bank, south bank; with each crossing of the broad river, Jim's hands grew dirtier with the feel of copper coins. Ink and paper from his roll of tickets added to the grime on his fingers, the palms of his hands, creeping up as far as his wrists. Rain clouds massed over Dumbarton Rock, which rose around the bend of the river like a fortified stud on the belt of antique stones round Scotland's waist – Dumbarton, Stirling Castle, Edinburgh Castle. The clouds were dark enough to warn of a summer downpour. It rained that day, and made the work miserable and wet. From the top deck, he saw Robertson and the girl under a tree.

On a Friday evening, having just been paid, Jim took a silver florin from his wage packet and dropped it into the girl's pouch as he passed her. A few seconds later, it bounced off the road in front of him. He saw it roll under a car. He turned round, but she already had her back to him and was shaking her cloth bag at the cars. Robertson noticed, too, but he kept on piping.

"How come," Jim asked his mother, "Robertson's daughter would throw back at me the florin I dropped into her bag? I thought we were well in with the tinkers. I mean, free eggs, and my father fixes them up with jobs."

"For someone who's supposed to have brains," said Mrs Gilchrist, "you're not very bright."

"She threw it back at me," he said angrily.

"Maybe she likes you," his mother said. "If I were a tinker lass whose father set her to begging off other folk and somebody I liked gave me a coin – more, maybe, than I was used to getting – then I think I'd throw it back." She smiled as she watched Jim thinking about what she'd said. "Don't do anything silly," she went on. "It'd be a great waste, you riding the length and breadth on a horse and cart."

"She's practically a next-door-neighbour, and I don't even know her first name. She hasn't said a word to me. It's not like how you think," he said. "I'd just been paid, and I felt generous."

"You so much as kiss her ear," his mother said, "and you'll wish you'd been stolen by the fairies. You, me, and your dad would find ourselves at a tinker's wedding – yours. They might look like nothing on earth, but they're very strict when it comes to what might be flitting across your mind."

Throughout the remainder of the summer, Jim thought about how to speak to the girl. She seemed able to guess whenever he came close to working up the courage. Blank as her expression looked, it was an emptiness that had been brought up on conventions of hostility, and that prepared her for the exercise of that gruff, rude dignity with which she snubbed and avoided him. Every few days, he joined the Robertsons at their fire as they sipped their strong tea. The girl said nothing, and her father did not think it discourteous when she walked away to stand by herself.

"Where did you learn to play?" Jim asked the man.

"My uncle taught me. He was a famous piper. Much better than my father was." Robertson groaned as he stood up. "I can huff and puff like the big bad wolf," he said, "but it's hard on the legs."

At the far end of the clearing, the girl counted the coins in her bag. Robertson doused the fire with what was left of his tea. He picked up his pipes and walked away. Before she followed him, the girl scuffed a foot's-worth of leaf mould on to the sizzles of the fire. She didn't even look at Jim. He felt inferior.

"Shy, aren't you?" said Ashton, back at the boat. "Tongue-tied and bashful. You slow down, she gives you a bad look, and then she gets on wi' her begging. A beggar's what she is, isn't it? Don't you know it? She's as far away from your own kind as a duchess or Lady Mucky-Muck. Will you buy a ticket for a good cause?" He was selling raffle tickets for the Scotland-USSR Friendship Society. "First prize is a week in Leningrad."

"What's the second prize?"

"If that's your attitude, then you don't deserve the opportunity of a lifetime which a possible prize-winning ticket would put your way."

"I suppose Poles and Hungarians get free tickets?"

"Counter-revolutionary trash gets what's coming to it, and that's what *it* gets. Forget it," Ashton said. "I can see I'm wasting time."

On the morning that Robertson's band of tinkers were to leave for their autumn and winter camp, Jim turned up for work an hour early, at half-past six. Ashton was already on board. He scowled at Jim.

"What've I done wrong this time?" Jim asked.

"Nothing." Ashton gave a shrug of innocence, his mouth opening, his teeth shining, amusement slowly drawing over his face. A late-September breeze nudged at Jim's cap as three tugs in a line went downriver. "It's your last day, an' I'll be glad to see the back of you. It'll no' be like last year, or the year before. When you cross here in the morning to catch your bus to the university, don't expect any favours when it comes to your fare."

"I've never heard you laugh, Ashton. When did you last laugh, like a normal person?"

"I laugh when I see a loser. I'm laughing right now."

There was no sign of Robertson's convoy on the road. Jim said, "The tinkers are crossing this morning. You listen, Ashton, and you listen good. They're going across, and no fares. If you make an issue of it, you'll wish you hadn't bothered."

"So that's why you got here before the early-duty car man. Sorry to disappoint you," Ashton said. He pointed to horse dung on the car deck. One of the piles had been trodden by heavy tyres. "You being the Tinkers' Friend, I was waiting on you to clean it up. They went through here a good half-hour ago." Ashton dragged on his cigarette, and his smoke trailed in the wind. "Three horse-drawn vehicles, one lorry, eighteen passengers, six of whom were half-fare, them being under-age. You're the man wi' the brain. You can tot that up in a flash, no bother, I'm sure. When did I laugh last? I've been laughing all morning. Here," he said, handing Jim a shovel. "Go and clean up what they left you."

"Are you sure it was them?"

"I've been here since 1933. Would I not recognize them? I looked forward to telling that scabby piper no' to come back, him and his mangy clan. They're redskins, jumping the reservation. Sure I'm sure. I'd know them a mile away. Why do you think I got here early?"

The wash of a freighter slapped against the ferry and ran over the car deck. Withdrawing waves swept it clean. Jim handed the shovel back to Ashton.

"Where are you going now?" Ashton shouted.

"Up for'ard," Jim shouted back, "to wait for your brother. Full fare!"

PHOTOGRAPHS OF STANLEY'S GRANDFATHER

"Your family must be very proud of him," I said, as Stanley struggled with his large parcel. He had just collected it from the picture framer's, and I had bumped into him at the corner nearest the shop. He balanced it on the low wall from which rise the immutable iron railings which surround the public park.

"I told you," he said. "It's strong stuff, this paper. I knew it would be no trouble." He had insisted on showing the photograph to me, on the spot. He licked the last strip of sticking paper, that strong stuff, and pieced the brown-paper parcel together again. It was about three feet long by two-and-a-half feet wide. "They do an excellent job," Stanley said.

"Yes. I'll bear them in mind." We strolled along the side of the park. Rhododendrons bulged against the iron bars with their dry, dusty greens. "Are you sure you wouldn't like me to carry that?" I asked. It was visibly awkward for Stanley to fit that flat, rectangular package under his short, thin arm. Anyone who's carried such a parcel knows how difficult it can be. He was determined to carry it by himself.

Neither Stanley nor myself is, as they say, in gainful employment. In my case, I am convalescing from a chronic condition of the lungs, and Stanley is dying. At thirty-two you can be dying and know it. For as long as I've known Stanley, which is all my life, he's been dying. There is a secret likelihood I am on the edge of my own decease. Only a few weeks before I had been told that my condition would be permanent. Too much fine Saharan sand on my last contract – Wonderful, I thought; I've never smoked in my life and now I'm a cripple with broken breath. In my private annals, I am the man who should have been more careful, who should have spared himself and been in less of a hurry to get that infernal project well and truly established before the Moroccan inspectors – lazy, expatriate Frenchmen in any case – turned up to ensure that their government was not pouring its money into a foreign maw. As for Stanley, he has never worked in his life. His health was too delicate for him to be sent to school. It is difficult to feel he has so much as a nationality. He is, to use a genealogical term, issue; he lives in the lap of his family. A malady of the blood, they say, is destined to finish him off, but they've been saying that for years.

"How about your family, Stan? Are they conscious of having come down in the world? I mean, I imagine they might be. It's just a question," I said, defensively. He looked at me as if I had chosen to put the most indiscreet remark possible. "Mine were certainly conscious of having come *up*," I said, trying, as light-heartedly as I could manage, to be self-effacing. "Other than my mother, of course. I suppose she thought of herself as settling down on her expected level." Stanley did his best to shrug while holding that capriciously geometric bundle. "I'm not trying to insult you. Your grandfather was a living legend, but neither your father nor yourself could be said to have made much of a mark on the world."

"Some people, people like my grandfather," said Stanley, "are destined to begin things. People like my father are destined to inherit them. It's as simple as that."

"Then your grandfather doesn't cast an embarrassing shadow?"

"My father hardly ever mentions him, actually."

"I really think you ought to give that to me," I said.

"No," he protested, "it's all right. I can manage it." He balanced the picture on his knee, halfway to transferring its weight and shape to his other side.

We crossed the main road and put the park behind us as we entered the streets of the district in which we both live. An air of stone-faced gentility becomes palpable as soon as you meet these streets. Other than the evidence of a few parked cars, you would think no one lives in these houses. Respectable frontages, those obsessively neat gardens, announce that the residents here do not speak to just anyone. From time to time I find it difficult to believe they actually speak to each other. A thick, leafy sobriety, a summer silence, hung in the mid-afternoon air and there was a warm wind.

Stanley lives with his parents, cocooned in ancestral sandstone. I was born here. My brother is demanding that I take steps to sell the house, as is my sister. We own a third of it apiece, but only I live there and I will for as long as I can continue to trade on their pity. I use it to hold off their greed and to postpone my own decisions. My standard argument is financial, that is, that the house is constantly increasing in value the longer we keep it. At the beginning, they were impressed by this for neither is in need of funds. After all they are the children of my father, and one is a doctor and my sister is married into comfort. Ready money, however, is now a more preferable objective than their brother's hapless security.

"I can see how a famous man in a family would give you something to hang on to," I said. "It must mean a lot to you."

"Don't tease me," Stanley said.

"*Tease you*?"

"Everyone knows how interested I am in my grandfather. I happen to believe that his work amounts to a very considerable achievement."

"Of course, it was a very considerable achievement indeed. Donaldson Park," I said. "Apart from anything else, it isn't everyone who has a public park named after his grandfather. Conscientiousness is not," I said, "a quality I scoff at. I can claim to have been conscientious myself, although all it did for me was put sand in my anatomy. Stanley," I said, "if that had happened last century, or by about 1910 at the latest, then my condition would have been considered a tragedy in the service of Good Works. It would have been hymned as martyrdom to the benefits which irrigation brings to backward peoples. But now all it amounts to is a minor contention in the history of insurance. Sand," I said, "sand, so fine, so very fine, Stanley, that you can't even see it. Finer than dust."

"You must have been vulnerable from the start."

"What?"

"Going there," he said, "from a humid country like this, to one so dry. You were probably liable."

We walked on in silence for a few minutes. I coughed, hoping, deliberately, to bring him round to the subject of me.

"There's to be another book about him," Stanley said, once again transferring the framed photograph to another hand.

"Why don't you roll your sleeves up and write a book yourself?"

"A book like that," he said, "would take years. One would have to travel a lot, too, to libraries, to interview people. Besides, I know too much."

"Scandal?"

"Disappointed as I must be to have to agree with you," he said, in spurts, the object in his hand beginning to have almost a life of its own, "yes, scandal; but hardly the sort of thing that would reach the headlines."

"Then it must be financial," I said, "and not sexual."

"Sexual? Good God, no, nothing like that. Your own father must have a skeleton in his cupboard, I'll bet."

"Stanley," I said, "my father *is* a skeleton in a cupboard." We walked on. The hill was gradually becoming steeper. The suburb is built around a hill, and the best houses are at the top. "How long was he a Member of Parliament?"

"Less than a year. He got in on a bye-election. He was terribly influential by then but the general consensus is that he was never suited to the political life. They say he turned his coat afterwards, but his principles didn't change in the least."

"Are you honestly sure you don't want me to take that now?"

"No. I can manage it. I've told you, I can do it."

"How many pictures do you have?"

"When I can afford it, I get the better ones framed. As for how many, I suppose I have about fifteen. No," he said, correcting himself, "I'm forgetting this one. Sixteen. Yes, sixteen."

The road began to climb steeply through the groves and avenues of the respectable and towards the peak of the suburb. Glasgow is thought to be a classic among cities founded upon poverty and drunken impertinence. That may be true enough but it is also a turbine on the factory floor of middle-class engineering, a power-house in the production of respectability. We did not talk on this part of our journey. Every few paces I had to stop and catch my breath. When I walked I had to lean myself against the incline and take it steadily. Stanley moved with relentless lethargy. As soon as we crossed the next deserted road – no stray dogs, no children, no housewives with shopping-bags, only a few parked cars which snarled threateningly through arrogant radiator teeth – as soon as we had crossed it, Stanley, ahead of me, stopped and placed his precious photograph against a low wall. He sat on the wall and loosened his tie. The wall had recently been washed and smelled of soap. Grown men, sitting on a wall, are, in that district, good cause for the inhabitants to wonder at which strangers have entered their pious suburb.

"This," he said, "this can't be good for you. It's your lungs, isn't it?"

"Why do I do it? I climb this every day. I should remember to get a taxi. I ought to buy a car. And you don't look too brilliant either."

"I've a researcher coming at four," Stanley said, looking at his watch. Sweat on his pale brow looked like a thinner water than sweat, as he wiped his face with his sleeve. "It's the man who's writing the next book. Remarkably well thought of, and, in fact, he's made several extremely valuable contributions to industrial history. I'm looking forward to it."

"Then press on," I said, "but I wish to God you'd suggested a taxi. Now will you give me an end of that thing? It's beating you into the ground."

Not expecting to be refused, I took hold of one end of the flat bulk which Stanley was trying to load under his arm. Its edges had already made red scores on his wrists. I could imagine the exact sensations of strain and discomfort on his upper arms which carrying an object of that shape and size would have created. He resisted, and, as I tugged, and as he tugged in the opposite direction, a swathe of brown paper came away in our hands. That sticking tape he had referred to with inane pride as "strong stuff" had not been as tough as he thought. A flap of paper waved in the oppressively warm wind. Presented to us both was a self-confident smile, that sly, calculating, monochromatic stare of Stanley's grandfather.

It was the look of a leader of men. The old boy looked in excellent health. A thick carpet of whiskers flourished on his upper lip. His eyes were clear, his eyebrows were copious and were obviously fair in colour; his cheeks were drawn, his collar was loose on his thin neck, and his chin looked fleshless. It was an appearance of hedonistic gauntness, the look of a man who had at one time denied himself much in order to reach a position where he need deny himself nothing. Stanley's grandfather looked a formidable opponent. He was, I guessed, in his mid-fifties and therefore at an age which Stanley might never reach, that is if Stanley is dying as certainly as is taken for granted. There is a chance he has been pampered into a state of physical and spiritual incompetence but that, I suppose, is also to be dying or it is at the least the next best thing.

My disengagement from our pathetic little struggle – I heard the quiet grunts and heaves of two invalids, and felt childish and ashamed – caused a dramatic imbalance in Stanley's grip. The framed photograph tilted across his chest and slid towards the pavement. Only my quick intervention stopped it from falling.

"Leave it to me," he snapped, angrily.

"Suit yourself," I said.

He got down on his knees and did his best to reorganize the torn wrapping paper. I got down beside him and tried to help. He slapped my hand away. "Fine," I said. "Right. You're on your own." I took a couple of steps back.

"Look, I'm sorry. But I can do this by myself. I can at least take a picture to the framer's, and bring it back, can't I? I can be allowed to do *that*?"

"Stanley, carrying something that size up Park Hill is a job of work. A labourer would know he'd earned his wages after climbing Park Hill with that in his hands. I know. I used to employ them."

Fulminating in silence, he covered the face of his grandfather with what was left of the paper, as if it had been a more embarrassing nakedness. Soon the features of that nominator of a public park, of swimming baths, were hidden from view. Once again that notable industrialist became no more than a parcel.

Stanley left me a few minutes later. He had further to climb, towards the summit of Park Hill where his grandfather had built his number-two house. It is an Italianate stone villa, handsome, robust, dignified and plain.

Looking down, over that solid, staunch and disquietingly respectable suburb, ominously clean and where silence is an obligation, I thought it was more than likely that only the trees in this world are not an anachronism, or the swallows, which I have seen in winter, in Morocco.

KILBINNIN MEN

Every working day, Monday to Friday, and most Saturday mornings, and on the occasional Sunday, C. E. McColl drives past the village of Kilbinnin. To have been born there – to have been born in the functional, plain village that he sees from the main road as he drives by – is a source of pride for C. E. McColl. He is the sort of man who gathers relevant data about his birthplace, even though he left it at the age of nine. Knowing all there is to know about Kilbinnin, he is well aware that Fergus Smith, the internationally acclaimed architect, was born there.

Fergus Smith is now at the helm of a large, prosperous concern with worldwide connections. He was born ten years before C. E. McColl, and this fact, McColl tells himself as he drives past Kilbinnin, explains why McColl cannot remember Fergus or any other member of the Smith family. The satisfaction of having been born in Kilbinnin and therefore, naturally, knowing Fergus Smith has been denied to C. E. McColl, has been blocked, as it were, by time – by, as he calls it, that rudderless progression which nonetheless moves in a straight path.

The case of Bruce Murchison, the painter, is a different one entirely. He is one year older than C. E. McColl. Because of this proximity of birthdays, McColl reckons he must have known him. That he cannot put a face to Murchison, or recollect any Murchison episode, is, he has decided, just one of these quirks of time, that comprehensive non-substance which goes everywhere and is nothing but which moves in a set forward motion as neatly as McColl tears his electricity bill along the perforated line.

Kilbinnin was a smaller village when C. E. McColl lived in it. It is still a small village. He must have played with Bruce Murchison in the field that is still there, worn down to bare earth by the repeated advances and retreats of football. He can remember the field with excessive vividness. Strongly impressed

111

on his memory is the sensation of falling flat on his face in a muddy puddle at the goalmouth. But when he says the name "Bruce" to himself, or speaks it aloud as he is driving past Kilbinnin, it feels strange on his lips, as if it is a new word to him, spoken for the first time.

But he went to primary school in Kilbinnin. What they taught there laid the foundations of his later educational achievements. None of his teachers' names come back to him, but he can read, write, and add. Thinking about the village school brings the name of John Trento, the half-Italian, into his mind – Professor John Trento, that is, of a Canadian university, a specialist in abstruse areas of mathematics, most of which he seems to have pioneered at a very young age. McColl thinks that he ought to remember someone who must have been conspicuously clever even in primary school – and John Trento is about the same age as McColl, so he must have been in the same class, or the year above, or the year below. When he saw Professor Trento on television, speaking about the applications of his most famous theory to the American space programme, what he heard was a Canadian accent clumsily overlaid on a west of Scotland original. Face, voice, mannerisms – none of these were familiar. As hard as he tried, the closest McColl could get to a memory of John Trento was a Latin-looking face with the set expression of a goalkeeper at a moment of crisis dancing purposively between two sets of jackets, and seen by someone staring up from a muddy puddle.

Glad as he is to be identified with Kilbinnin and its famous sons, C. E. McColl is well aware that this is an association no one other than himself is likely to consider of any importance. He is not famous; but then he is not a failure, either. In his early forties, he is at the age when he knows he has failed to seize opportunities with the decisiveness that is a condition of success in modern life. Steady progress – that is the phrase to describe McColl's career. Each promotion has been a year or two late in materializing. Still, each step up the ladder has been taken, in the end. As manager of the firm's factory in the west of Scotland, he anticipates that one of these fine days he will be invited to take command of the company's entire operation in Scotland. No one, so far as he knows, and he does not think about it, has an active dislike of him. His staff, for example, consider him a pleasant plodder who, in these difficult times, will do his best to see that they don't lose their jobs. McColl has never perpetrated a single blunder that he has not been able to rescue from visible ineptitude – not in the intricate field of budgetary control, or even in the more difficult area of industrial relations. More and more, though, these recuperations are becoming last-minute salvations – very small shares indeed of foggily bounding time, creeping ever onward.

Henry Fraser is another famous product of the Kilbinnin Primary School. An actor, he is not of the top flight but a frequent performer in television series. His reputation is higher in theatrical circles than with the viewing public. "He was born in Kilbinnin," says McColl in front of his TV. His wife smiles and carries on knitting socks for her aged father. Their eldest son is fifteen. Fathers at McColl's age are susceptible to being detected as experts in the craft of repeating themselves. "My God, Dad, we *know*. You say that *every* time he's on." "Well, it's the truth," says McColl, "and if there's one thing that time neither clarifies nor destroys, it's the truth." Impatient with oracles, McColl's eldest son leaves the room.

The time came when there was a need for an engineer to replace a man who had been struck down by a coronary attack on the first day of the personnel manager's holidays. C. E. McColl applied by telephone to the employment agency. He asked to be sent details about anyone who might be suitable. Then he went to express his condolences in person to the unfortunate widow.

Two days later, after the funeral, McColl sat at his desk in his funeral suit looking through the forms from the employment agency. On one form a man called Felix Kennedy had given his place of birth as Kilbinnin, and the date of it as the fourth of August 1934. The man was exactly one month younger than McColl, born in the same parish. Kennedy? he asked himself. *Felix* Kennedy? McColl thought he should remember someone called *Felix* Kennedy, someone whose unusual first name must have made his life a misery. He couldn't. He had left Kilbinnin when he was nine. Nine years, he thought, is long enough to have gathered memories. What vague, always happy memories he had could not have arisen from nowhere. A childhood that fails to provide memories of other children is not a satisfactory childhood. He wished his parents were still alive so he could phone them and be reminded of this phenomenon of his childhood that he seemed to have lost somewhere, like the dry-cleaning ticket he had left inside a library book. Felix Kennedy? *Felix*? He could no more remember Felix Kennedy than he could Fergus Smith, Bruce Murchison, Professor John Trento, or Henry Fraser. These days Henry Fraser was appearing by courtesy of the Royal Shakespeare Company. Clearly, he was on the verge of a breakthrough. One big success and he would be a name, someone it would be improper to have forgotten.

Two days later, Felix Kennedy arrived for an interview as requested. While Kennedy was waiting in the outer office, McColl was on the phone to his masters in London. A forecast of production figures had to be explained to them, because the figures were embarrassingly higher than head office had bargained for. He was being congratulated and asked to double-check. He had already double-checked. Several people had double-checked his double-checking.

Elated by this triumph of reliability and thoroughness, McColl asked for Kennedy to be sent into his office. Nothing in Felix Kennedy's appearance was familiar, but McColl had already suspected that nothing would be. He could not see the child Kennedy in the man, who was a tall, well-built individual.

"I see you're a Kilbinnin man," said McColl.

"Yes, I was born there," said Kennedy.

"I was born there myself," said McColl, glancing back at the application form in an attempt to be casual and not give away the eagerness of his curiosity, which he doubted – and still doubts – anyone else could understand, because it is not understandable to him. "Born, in fact, in the July of 1934," he added, with a smile. "On the fourth of July."

"McColl?" asked Felix Kennedy.

"Yes. 'C', for Colin."

"Colin McColl?" the man ruminated. "Where in Kilbinnin?"

"Dyce Crescent," said McColl, "Number ten."

"Oh, I see. We lived on the other side of the village, in the older part – next door to Murchison, in fact. You'll remember Bruce. He was about the same age as us."

McColl said in a sideways nod that he didn't.

"McColl? Wait a minute. Did your father have a car?"

"He did, as a matter of fact. It was a Vauxhall."

"I remember you. Colin McColl, eh? Well, it's a small world. One minute you're a boy, and the next you're on the labour market. In no time at all, no time at all."

"We were looking for a qualified man," said McColl, "but I see you've the kind of *experience* we want. Experience counts for a lot here."

"I hope so," said Kennedy, light-hearted about his lack of job. "It's six months since I've worked."

"I was sorry to see them close," said McColl. "It was too bad – a firm as long established, and as well respected . . . It shouldn't happen."

"These things are beyond our control."

"You served your time there, too, I see."

"Qualifications," said Kennedy. "It won't be the first time I've been turned down for the lack of a piece of paper, Colin," he said good-humouredly. "But I'm sure I can do the job."

McColl smiled at this use of his Christian name. "It's a funny thing," he said. "I keep trying, but I can't place you in Kilbinnin. You see, my family moved when I was nine."

"You can't?"

"No," said McColl sadly. "I can't remember Bruce, either."

"You've heard about how well he's done, though?"

"Oh, yes, of course. Extremely well."

"I'm no judge of an oil painting myself," said Kennedy, "but they tell me he's one of the best and that what he does is highly appreciated from the financial point of view as well. His folks are still there, you know, next door to mine. Well, my mother died a year ago, and my father's not in the best of health. Mr and Mrs McColl still alive, Colin?"

"Both dead, I'm afraid."

"I'm sorry to hear that."

"About the qualifications . . ."

"It's not the first time," said Kennedy, trying to make rejection easier for McColl.

"What I was thinking," said McColl, "is that Kilbinnin men ought to stick together." Kennedy smiled. "That is, if you can give me your personal guarantee that I won't regret it."

"Smoke?" offered the new employee.

"No, thanks, I don't."

"Mind if I do, Colin?"

"No, go ahead."

Felix Kennedy lit up and inhaled. "I'm grateful, Colin. I'm grateful to you."

"It's quite a place, Kilbinnin," said McColl. "An architect . . . ?"

"Fergus Smith?"

"By all accounts a leader in his field. And an artist, a painter of outstanding merit, already the subject of an expensive book. I've seen it, in Smith's bookshop in St Vincent Street."

"It makes me feel proud to have known him," said Kennedy, "in the days when he was still struggling for recognition. He gave me a painting, you know."

"You own a *Murchison*?"

"Oh, yes. Oh, yes, Colin."

"Felix, I'm jealous."

"Don't forget wee John, Colin. That man might be the worst goalkeeper who ever worked out a sum, but there's no denying it, there's a man of genius for you – *Professor* John Trento."

"And Henry Fraser, an actor whose Macbeth, they tell me, will be the sensation of the London stage."

"Aye – Harry. You know, of course, that Harry Fraser's a fairy."

"I didn't know that. But live and let live, Felix. It makes no difference to me. Was he in our class?"

"A year before us, Colin. You haven't done too badly yourself. This is a very nice office."

McColl smiled and thought of how Felix Kennedy would go back to Kilbinnin, to his father whose health was bad, and tell them that C. E. McColl – remember him? – was a big wheel in the Scottish operation of a world-famous brand name, with a very nice office and with prospects, surely, in that future towards which time, bearing along as it did so many talents and destinies, was ruthlessly headed.

"Then I'll expect you to start on Monday, if that's acceptable."

"I'll look forward to it, Colin."

"Good. John, you said, played in goal, is that right?"

"Couldn't be trusted on the field," said Kennedy with a laugh. "Couldn't be trusted in goal, either, if you remember," he added.

"Yes, I remember that."

McColl wanted to ask where he himself played but felt that the question might sound strange. They shook hands. "Well, Felix, as one Kilbinnin man to another, congratulations."

Every day of his working week, C. E. McColl drives past Kilbinnin, where he was born. He knows from Felix Kennedy that he, Felix, Bruce, John, and Harry all played together. They did. Piece by piece, his memories are being made for him by his employee. He has met Mrs Kennedy, a Kilbinnin woman, who also remembers him. Getting around to remembering the Kilbinnin girls, though, still lies before him. McColl still feels his good luck is insubstantial – he is a realistic, unsentimental man, who is going back in time as well as forward, swept along in its cumulative tides. The Kennedys have been to dinner at the McColls'. Talk of Henry Fraser shut his son's mouth on that subject for ever. Now that Felix's parents are both dead, he has taken over the family home. As soon as he has finished the necessary redecorating and modernization, the McColls will go for dinner there, next door to the Murchisons.

THE TENNIS COURT

Polish officers freewheeled down that long hill in the early evenings. High-spirited men arrived first, whooping and shouting and waving their racquets. There were often two to a bicycle. More mournful, more conservative individuals followed them with judicious pressure on their brakes, as if they had not mastered the exhilarations of downhill bicycle-riding. Half an hour later those who preferred to walk would stroll through the village with their polite "Good evenings" and little bows. Our parents told us it was wonderful how these Poles could be pleasant to strangers when they had so much on their minds. Like the others, those who came on foot were dressed in as many bits and pieces of tennis clothes as they could lay their hands on. Some wore white slacks or white shorts and military shirts or sweaters. Others wore military shorts or drill trousers and white shirts or white sweaters. Only one or two possessed a complete white ensemble. Members of the Tennis Club presented them with what discarded whites they could, rather as head waiters keep a tie or two for those gentlemen thoughtless enough to arrive without one.

For two or three hours, on one or two evenings a week, the court seemed possessed by Polish players. Their excitable Polish language was shouted around while the sedate but tolerant members of the Club looked on or chatted with non-playing senior officers, who behaved as if they had made a point of being there to keep an eye on the younger officers of the regiment. Ladies of the Club chirruped as their hands were kissed, a gallant custom which, alas, has fallen into disuse on these islands. I distinctly remember a young woman protesting. "But he's so dashing, Daddy! And he's been through so much!" She was petulant, but her father was extremely cross. "He may be as dashing as fifty VCs put together," he said, with that dismissive but carefully controlled rage of which only the male parent is capable, "and for all I care, he can have been through Hell. But you will not see him again!"

Men found themselves stuck for words when these Polish officers presented them with "little presents" or brought flowers for their wives. One of them gave me a posy of wild flowers he had gathered on his way to the court. "A l'le girl," he said to my father, "shud hiv flo'rs. Blue flo'rs far blue ess. No? Yis, yis, *such* blue ess." "This little girl," said my mother, "is about ready for beddy-byes." I could have thrown a tantrum. I wanted to stay, and pose, with my wild bouquet, for I did not think of myself as little as all that and neither, I suspect, did my mother.

At dusk, the Polish officers pedalled back up that long hill to the commandeered mansion in which they were billeted. I saw them from my bedroom window. Sweaters, racquets, phrase-books, and other impedimenta, were balanced on the handlebars of their bicycles. Snatches of Polish conversation could be heard faintly from the pedestrian soldiers. I was fourteen at the time, but I still remember one last half-white figure disappearing into the darkening rhododendrons of Sir George Maclean's garden, one evening, when, as I heard from my father the following morning, that distinguished old soldier sent an invitation down to the court for the Poles to stop by his house for a drink.

British, Canadian and American fliers from the naval air base, sometimes from aircraft carriers anchored on the Clyde, came and played on our court. They arrived in an impressive miscellany of transport. Parked on the grass verge by the side of the road, there would be navy-blue cars driven by Wrens, jeeps, a truck or two, and sometimes a rakish sports car for our brothers to admire. Those dark blues were dappled in the evening sunlight as it filtered through the trees and penetrated the shadow cast by the high stone wall that masks the court from the road. That summer light on the vehicles made a colour that was memorable, which one would want to preserve. These airmen were high-spirited, too. They arrived in perfect attire. The Poles went first, in 1944. A year and a half later the court was ours again.

More tennis was played on our court in these last two summers of the war than at any time before or since. There was a tennis wedding in All Hallows in 1945. Arm-in-arm, under a salute of raised racquets, the American groom and his local bride smile on the fading newsprint in these bound volumes of the *Press & Advertiser* which anyone can leaf through in the Public Library in town. If they come from here, and do not feel like making the trip, then they can consult them in Mr Ferrier's attic, for he has the best part of a complete set.

That, then, was Miss Devorgilla Cunningham, made Mrs DeLancey O'Hara, of Boston, Mass. I was at the wedding. They return here from time to time, for Devorgilla's sister still lives in the family house of Craigenmun. Bella Cunningham is, I suppose, my one and only close friend. She is two years older then me, so I play against her, and, on those rare occasions when we can make up the numbers for a game of doubles, I play with her. As a combination, we are unbeatable locally. We are both spinsters. I do not like that word, but I am stuck with it. Bella is fifty-two, and I am fifty although you would not think it to look at me. For us both, tennis, and the Tennis Club, are large occupations and not to be taken lightly. I am the daughter of a Professor of Gynaecology, one of those earnestly amiable Scottish physicians of which the world, perhaps, has known too many. His vigorous but incompetent exertions on our tennis court fell into the category of once witnessed, never forgotten. He would justify his disastrous drives, his ungainly balletics and hopeless leaps and bounds, by saying, "It's all exercise anyway. What, after all, is tennis, if not a form of exercise?" He did not play tennis so much as keep fit. As a consequence of his reputation, no one – and they should have known better – took my tennis seriously until I had made it my business to win the Junior Ladies County Championship. Bella Cunningham lifted that same trophy the year before. Two years younger than she on that moment of triumph, I can be said to be one up on her where it matters. In our games against each other, the score, I regret to confess, stands at 354 matches to Bella, and 76 to me. To set against this shameful statistic, I must point out that we have been keeping this tally for only the past ten years. It is a lot of tennis, but we did not keep a record until we were past our best. Bella has a black notebook in which she records each game, each set, each match. Yes, it would have to be black.

Why, at my age, you may ask, do I continue to play such a competitive game of tennis? In reply, I contend that Bella does not beat me by all *that* much. She beats me regularly, indeed, but the scores are *close*. This, I cannot help but observe, puts Bella in a better light than it places me. Or so it will look to those who do not know the facts. Bella, after all, is fifty-two. Yes, you are right, should you consider our heroic duels absurd. It is rather worse for her at fifty-two. Isn't it? My birthday falls gratifyingly in the midst of our summer contests, on the 9th of July. "Bella," I said this year, and I was far from breathless, "I think I'll call it a day."

"Have you had enough, my dear?" She is not the sort of person who remembers her own birthday let alone that of her oldest friend.

"At my age," I said, "this is all quite ridiculous. I'm fifty, you know."

"You are forty-seven," she said. "And don't you forget it. I know, because I am forty-nine and you are two years younger."

This confused me. I am easily contradicted. Silently, I counted back to the year of my birth. "No," I said, "my birthday is today, and I'm fifty."

"Congratulations!" She left me at the net and took up position to resume her service. She shot a venomous ball at me that bounced accurately just inside the line and left me completely adrift. "Happy birthday, my dear!" Another of her militaristic wallops came at me.

"That was *out*!" It wasn't, but there is never any harm in trying.

If I may say so, I have kept my neck in a state far closer to a swanlike and sporting ideal than has Bella Cunningham. Mrs O'Hara's neck is the better for regular tennis, too, but I understand it is common practice in Boston, Mass., for expensive surgery to be performed upon perished skin, or sagging jaws. Apparently, a moment is reached when former beauties are forced to concede that the glassy information of their mirrors is the truth, after all, and that they must realize they have reached a matronly status. Or so I have heard.

As for my arms, then, these, I assure you, show no signs of

121

deteriorating into that flabby, non-youthful condition which is common to ladies of my age. Bella Cunningham's arms are vulgarly muscular. I have a sneaking suspicion she indulges in weightlifting. It is not that I have ever come across her heaving heavy metal about in whatever room in Craigenmun she uses as her secret gymnasium. I am going by that other evidence of my eyes, her sheer bulk. Manly exercises of that sort would certainly explain why it is that Bella Cunningham has a moustache.

And now, my legs. I am justifiably proud of my legs. At one time I considered them to be far and away my best feature. Indeed, I was for ever showing them off when young men were in the vicinity. Exercise has not made them too muscular. They are, I dare say, conspicuous for their beauty, as much as for the extent to which they portray me as a woman in excellent physical condition. Bella Cunningham shaves hers. I have deduced this from her hirsute armpits, the dark hair on her arms, and the five o'clock shadow beneath her nose. "Why, Bella," I have asked her, "must you insist on wearing such awfully young tennis outfits?"

"What? I thought this one was rather becoming."

I do not wish for one moment to be unfair to Bella, but I think I succeeded in afflicting her with some of that consternation and self-perusal of which she stood in serious need this summer, although my charitable nature did not permit me to be as candid towards her as I should have been. That has always been my predicament in my long friendship with Bella Cunningham. Shall I tell her what I really think of her? Shall I come clean, and speak to her, as one friend to another? It has always been like that. But in the past few years it has weighed on me like a responsibility. We are all to some extent responsible for our friends' behaviour. It is up to us to prevent them from looking ridiculous in the eyes of those who do not love us. "It's those frilly pants," I said. "All very well for Miss Wade, or Miss Navratilova, but I fear they do not quite suit Miss Cunningham."

"I do hope you are not suggesting," she said, and a negative, on the lips of Bella, when she's feeling haughty, is like a threat, "you are not suggesting that I have reached the age of *slacks*?"

"Not for one moment. But look at you. There is," I reminded her, "a kind of, well, a sort of 'bend' in your legs."

"Bend?" she looked down at her legs. "I am *not* bandy-legged!"

"Your knees," I pointed out, "do not touch when you stand to attention. Now do they?"

She drew her feet together and looked down. "They *don't*." I could not quite decide if her tone of voice was one of plaint, or one of defiance.

"What if someone should see you?"

"Who," she asked, "is likely to?"

Her answer had the effect of perplexing *me*. It was true, the Club is usually unpopulated. In a sense it is no longer a Tennis Club at all. The Macleans' gardeners keep it in good order, but this generosity on their part has come to look more like a special favour to us than to the Tennis Club. Twenty-two members we may have, on paper, but we hardly ever see them. The Club House is not what it was, but we keep it as clean and as adequate as we can. Fortunately, we can afford it. From time to time we have seen evidence of tennis having been played before our arrival at the court. Here and there, the odd soft-drinks can, trampled grass, a ball that is certainly not one of ours, a rolled Kleenex, give the show away. We cannot help but notice an uncouthly rolled net, flung any-old-how in a corner of the Club House. Enquiries made of the Macleans' gardeners inform us that so-and-so was there, young persons, taking advantage of their parents' member-ships. Keys are needed, one to unlock the gate in the wall, another to open the gate into the court itself, and a third for the Club House door. "Someone," I said, "may be walking his dog. And children often play in these woods. *Anyone* could see you."

"It's hardly changed. It seems just the same, doesn't it DeLancey?" Thus the former Devorgilla Cunningham to her husband, when they visited last year. It was an enchanting tennis reunion. The evening began with a gentle game between that couple from Boston, Mass. They looked like bride and groom again, setting off on the first waltz of married life. That court must mean so much to them. We all applauded with soft pats of the hand, although the standard of tennis was disgraceful. Several club members managed to drag themselves from their houses to be present. Friends of Devorgilla's, living elsewhere, turned up for the occasion. We had mixed doubles after the O'Haras finished their intimate, significant game. "Bella, for Heaven's sake, *must* you?" That was not me, for I am well used to Bella's barbaric serve, and that deeply-breathed, fiercesome squaring of her shoulders which precedes it, she of the barbels and calisthenics. Mrs O'Hara did her best, but gave up, claiming she was no longer a match for Bella's vindictive interpretation of the game. Nor was Mr O'Hara who, by the end of the evening, was, undoubtedly, in that "bad shape" to which he confessed. He was also in need of a recuperative lie-down, of which he promptly availed himself on our return to Craigenmun.

"I rather think," I said quietly to Bella, on the court that evening as the O'Haras played, "that you are suffering from envy."

"How odd," she said. "That's *exactly* what I thought I read on your face."

When our tennis season is over, we go on holiday together. For some years we have frequented Aix-en-Provence where tennis in September is rather fun. We were sitting, after dinner, having played a taxing game of doubles against two French ladies that afternoon. "I could hardly hold back the giggles when they said they were here for the Spa," I said.

"But surprisingly good players," said Bella.

"You played rather well," I said. Bella was suspicious of this compliment. "Such a pity they couldn't join us for dinner. It would be nice to play them again."

"They could never beat *us*," Bella said, which was satisfying.

"I do miss our own court when we're away," I said. "Don't you?"

"Yes, I do," she said, in that cold manner of hers whenever anything personal is brought up.

"Especially at this time of year, when the first leaves of autumn fall, and blow across it."

"You can be so sentimental about that court." Bella consulted the menu. People with appetites as hearty as Bella's like to reread the menu, *after* dinner, already looking forward to what they will have tomorrow. "No, you're right. I miss it at this time of year, too. I think of it as resting, as hibernating. And I don't know what there is to gloat over," she said, crossly, "just because I admit to an affection for our tennis court."

"I think these French ladies rather disliked us, by the end." It had been a hard-fought match. Bella chortled through her nose.

"My dear, I should think they detested us. I don't think they're used to being beaten."

I shared in this for a moment, then said, "I was not gloating, you know. I simply felt pleased that you should feel the same way as I do." My assurances did not seem to satisfy her. For years I had been wondering if I might go a little further in my exploration of our mutual fondness for our tennis court. Of course, I always knew what Bella felt, but she is not the sort of person who speaks her feelings. Allowances have to be made for her. I decided to press on. She was in a good mood, with a notable victory under her belt, not to mention an excellent dinner and several glasses of *Côtes d'Aix* vin rosé, which is to be recommended. "I have this wonderful memory of the Poles," I said. "Such unhappy, courteous and charming men. And of the Americans and the Canadians. Remember?"

"So?"

"I think you are so very like me," I said, "only you will never bring yourself to admit it." I thought she might bray at me with disbelief. Instead, she did not say anything; she merely shrugged. On such shoulders, broad shoulders, a shrug is expressive and very noticeable. We were ten days away from our own court – on which the grass was lengthening, leaves were browning – and I thought Bella would be in the mood to let me say what I wanted without chastisingly tut-tutting at every turn. "We want so much to go back to that time, don't we?"

"No one," she said, "ever goes back."

"No, I suppose not. But we would like to. That's the point, you see. Sometimes," I said, "it's crossed my mind that we're two ageing girls, hanging around that tennis court, in the hope of another war. Isn't that awful?" To my surprise, Bella was still listening, her head tilted slightly away from me. I expected her to tell me to shut up and not talk such rubbish. "And then the Poles would come down on their bicycles. There would be the Fleet Air Arm, the United States Navy, and the DeLancey O'Haras of this world. Anyway," I said, "I know it's silly of me, but that's what I feel. Sometimes," I added, because I did not want her to think that I felt like that very often. There is such a thing as discretion, even between very old friends. She bit her lower lip and managed to smile at the same time, with a little laugh. "And you?" I asked. That was the difficult question.

I thought she might cry, but I do not believe Bella could ever cry in a public restaurant. "Not often," she said. "Not often. But I sometimes feel like that too."

There. I had said it. And I was right. I don't know what people thought of us, if they saw me reach across the table, to hold Bella's hand, which I saw, was posed above the white linen, waiting.

WOMEN WITHOUT GARDENS

Sunlight on a bowl of apples on the table by the window encourages an appreciative smile from Mrs Ellison as she turns from her mirror where she has fussed her hair and her face. She smooths the tablecloth that completely covers the polished surface on which there are remarkably few heat-stains, burns or scratches for a table that has given such good and long family service. The cloth is necessary. Mrs Ellison is afraid that the sunlight would blanch the shine she rubs to perfection several times a week.

There is far from enough room in her small flat. She wishes there was somewhere more convenient where she could put her table and where, too, it could stand with its three remaining matching chairs. A corner of her heavy curtains does not hang properly but is bunched on the window-ledge. She tugs the lined brocade and the material settles in a perfectly weighted hang. She draws the curtains together by a few feet more and is hampered by the table's awkward position. At this time of the year the afternoon sun can fall on the damask antimacassars on her armchairs and sofa and draw out their whiteness. A last look round the room reveals her library book open on her armchair. She inserts her cloth bookmark on which a motto from Saint Augustine is stitched. *We must sing as we serve*, it says. Mrs Ellison thinks there is something wrong in closing a book on so agreeable an imperative.

She places the book on top of two other library novels which are sitting on the coffee-table many people have admired over the years. Its surface is an abstract design composed of hundreds of pieces of coloured ceramic. It was created by her youngest son when he was at the School of Art. Visitors say nothing about its design. Instead, they enthuse over the patience with which it has obviously been put together. As she pulls on her coat Mrs Ellison frowns as the little pile of novels catches a corner of her eye. She has read everything by the authors who please her most. So few books seem left for her to read. When something new comes out by an author whose books she enjoys then she immediately enters her name for it on the library's waiting list. Two years ago the library announced that it was giving up its time-honoured practice of maintaining waiting-lists for books in demand. Mrs Ellison associated her name with the petition of protest that was drawn up. It is the only occasion on which she ever felt herself to be a member of anything other than her family. Once she has put on her hat, she re-examines her face in the mirror. She is sixty-seven years old and has been widowed for ten of them.

It is invariably the case that Miss Drewery is never ready when Mrs Ellison calls. Miss Drewery's appearance is strikingly different from that of her friend who waits for her. She is tall, lean and muscled while Mrs Ellison is of a much plumper construction. Tennis is the source of Miss Drewery's anecdotes and memories. Tennis is said to explain her lithe movements and her quick and observant eye. Her skin is dark and young. She looks weathered by a long succession of girl's summers. No one expects a lady of Miss Drewery's age to run with a long stride but Miss Drewery when standing still gives Mrs Ellison the impression that she is about to rush off like a sprinter should someone snap their fingers or a window slam shut. Most of the time she appears to be in a state of competition and intolerably fit. She can eat as much as she likes and never get fat, which Mrs Ellison envies, although she is also amused by the extent to which Miss Drewery behaves like an immature person. She has been inside Miss Drewery's flat on only three occasions. No wonder, she thought then, that Miss Drewery skimps on her invitations to tea. Her flat is a perfect disgrace. Her furniture is good, her curtains well made and of excellent material, and her carpets are delightful, but the trouble is Miss Drewery leaves newspapers and books lying around any old where, with coffee mugs, plates with crumbs, vases in which flowers are two days withered, while the surfaces of her furniture are always dusty.

More irritating is the intercom through which Mrs Ellison announces her arrival to Miss Drewery after she has rung the doorbell. Miss Drewery's bell is indicated by a metal nameplate. Other tenants are content with small squares of paper affixed by drawing-pins. A buzzer makes it clear the front door has been automatically unlocked and can be opened with a gentle push. Mrs Ellison steps into the hall feeling as bewildered as ever by labour-saving devices. Letters for tenants who leave for work before the post arrives, or for late-risers, or the negligent, lie on a small table beside a vase filled with tasteless plastic flowers. There is a mirror in a brass frame which continues downwards into an expanse of unpolished brass from which four small hooks stick out. The brass-backed coat-brushes which presumably belonged to this elaborate piece of furniture have long since been removed while there are no galoshes, umbrellas or walking-sticks in the part of the object which sits on the floor, only a banana skin someone has dropped there on his or her way out. Mrs Ellison hopes they did not drop it there on the way *in*. That would be unforgivable.

After Miss Drewery has come downstairs, taking two steps at a time and landing at Mrs Ellison's feet with a thud, they leave together and collect Mrs Sinclair who lives several doors further along the avenue. She watches for Mrs Ellison entering Miss Drewery's front door. Once she is inside, Mrs Sinclair, who has been ready for some time, comes out and waits on the pavement adjacent to the front door of the house where she rents her small flat. Mrs Sinclair's shortness of temper and general impatience are believed to go with her pugnaciously diminutive size and the disgruntlement with which she fails to accept the inconvenience of sharing a bathroom and kitchen with other tenants she refers to as The Complete Strangers. It is not Mrs Sinclair's house but she behaves as if it is, and she treats her fellow tenants as if they are unwelcome guests who have vastly overstayed their welcomes.

All three ladies are waiting for that slight infirmity which will one day lead their relatives to suggest that they now think seriously about moving into what they will call a Nursing Home. Miss Drewery is perhaps exempt from this anxiety. She has no relatives although she does have friends in places like Malvern and South Africa. She worries however at having no one to tell her when she should give up her independence.

They are of small but secure income. Mrs Sinclair and Mrs Ellison enjoy the benefits of provision made for them by their late husbands. It is an unspectacular provision in Mrs Sinclair's case. She is acutely conscious of being unable to afford somewhere better to live. Miss Drewery has a higher income that the others. For years she was a private secretary to a succession of managing directors. Superannuation, cautiously administered, has left her high and dry and well enough off to afford two holidays in the year.

On the rainless days of summer they promenade the long avenues in which they live. It is a district of large houses. Many of them have come down in the world. A large number have been divided into apartments covering the complete price range. A few detached and substantial houses are still in the hands of people of quite considerable means, or the respectability to give that impression. Their gardens are the ones spared the daily assessments of these three ladies, Mrs Ellison, Mrs Sinclair and Miss Drewery. All the others are marked out of ten.

Many old ladies can be seen in this district in summer, on the dry pavements, walking together. Younger people can be seen in T-shirts and some young men in those abruptly casual shorts made by snipping a pair of jeans across the thighs with a pair of scissors. Mrs Ellison and Mrs Sinclair look on this style with a good deal of suspicion. To Miss Drewery it is *sportif* – her word. But she, too, admitting her age, wears a light summer coat, a straw hat, carries a handbag and wears white gloves although less consistently than her friends. Mrs Sinclair always wears white gloves. She is relieved when Miss Drewery does not wear gloves. Miss Drewery is forever breaking pieces of chocolate in her handbag and the way she smears her gloved fingers and then tries to wipe them on the palm of a gloved hand is like the behaviour of someone who has never worn gloves before in her life, which is to say nothing of how Miss Drewery looks in her bag with furtive delight and smacks her lips. Mrs Sinclair is adept at giving the impression Miss Drewery is not with her, but has been bumped into and will soon be gone in a different direction.

The pace of their walk is very slow. They pay attention to the gardens and you cannot inspect anything at speed. It is not unknown for Miss Drewery to break into a run and then come back to Mrs Ellison, who is too amused to know how to take such athletic behaviour, and Mrs Sinclair who scowls at Miss Drewery as if she is already too close to becoming one of The Complete Strangers. From the slowness of their walk you can tell when they are admiring a garden; and, too, you do not need to see the expressions on their faces when the same speed suggests that they are being highly critical. "Oh, do look at *that!*" one of them may exclaim and point out the delicious smudge of a lilac at the rear of a garden seen in a space between two houses. Sight of a garden shed with its door open, a lawnmower standing ready for the shove, or a man with his back to her putting earth in a seedbox, reminds Mrs Ellison of a garden that was once hers behind a house that for years was never quite big enough and which one day became suddenly too large for her to manage. Mrs Sinclair does not look sensitive enough to have such memories, but she has them anyway, although never in public. In the evening, after she has switched off a television programme that is of no interest or which is calculated to offend her, she drifts away on the silence.

They hold fierce opinions on gardens as neglected as the tufted squares of grass that front the houses they live in. Fortunately, all three live at the front of their houses, overlooking the street. They are spared views of the angeringly overgrown gardens at the back. Horticultural disasters tend to come in batches of several together. You can hear the tut-tut of their indignant points of view like the stamping of small, infuriated feet.

Miss Drewery has been known to say, "Yes, I know. They really *should* do something about it." "*Students,*" Mrs Sinclair interrupts with a sneer. "Oh, but not always. Even some quite respectable people just don't have the *time*." Mrs Sinclair resumes her derision by pointing out that it has nothing to do with time. It is a question of principle. By now they know that Mrs Sinclair's favourite word is about to be used. "It is a matter of *inclination*." Mrs Sinclair is convinced people are no longer *inclined* to do as they ought, to behave in the way they used to behave. And Mrs Ellison agrees with her. All her life she has agreed for the sake of avoiding the unpleasantness of an argument. At moments like this, she points towards something nice – a new coat of paint on a fence, a show of flowers – knowing Mrs Sinclair will approve and that inspecting it and reckoning up the marks due to it will either change the subject or shut Mrs Sinclair up.

One garden is their particular delight. They have gone so far as to confess to its middle-aged owner that he has been awarded ten marks out of ten. He has been off work since Christmas on account of his chest. The doctor encourages him to keep up with the light labour it takes to keep his garden the way he wants it. Mrs Ellison considers it admirable that he should persevere through thick and thin so affably when it would be easy to let things slip. They are concerned for his health. A finicky attention has been paid to every blade of grass on the small lawn in front of his house. It reminds Miss Drewery of the Centre Court at Wimbledon before the first day's play. A neighbour's laburnum hangs yellow on its massy gallows. It is more yellow than yellow itself.

Today the gardener is watering some small plants in a weedless border. Water descends and spreads in thin, delicate sprays from his can. They greet him and his sad, thoughtful expression changes to another which shows he is pleased to see them. Then he shows them a large white rose of which he is extremely proud. "It's so *early* for it to be so *large*," Mrs Sinclair says with emotion. She knows a thing or two about roses and her expertise makes her admiration of this one impressive. He tilts it gently towards them with his hand. It bows in homage.

Once this pleasant interlude is over, they walk further on, as satisfied as judges who have just given full marks to a competitor in the Olympic figure-skating championships. The nice old man in the linen jacket who walks his dog stops for a brief moment. He shares in their admiration of a squarely barbered privet hedge and their disappointment at the recent uncertainty of the weather. They also observe together and with some pleasure that the quite nice young man who really *ought* to do his garden more often has, in fact, done it, and quite thoroughly. If they could catch sight of him at his window, they would smile, all, that is, except Mrs Sinclair, who isn't too sure, and who suspects that in a month's time it will be as weedy as ever.

They make their customary remarks on how nice that old man is. Mrs Sinclair says his dog is so well-behaved it is the only dog she can imagine putting up with in the house. There is little conviction in the way she says it, but Miss Drewery knows what she means. Mrs Sinclair spots a wildly untutored hedge which after the recent rain has shot up to a variety of rugged heights. It is too high for them to see through to the front windows of the house and shame its owner.

Their destination is a public park. Before they arrive there, Mrs Ellison is already wondering about what time is most suitable for her to ask if Miss Drewery and Mrs Sinclair would like to come back to her flat for a cup of tea. She likes to know well in advance. Everything is already prepared. Immediately after her light lunch, she set cups and saucers on a tray as she always does. But she likes to sit in the park and think of what biscuits are in the tin and to picture her china in their hands. What causes her slight perplexity is that she feels it is only considerate to Miss Drewery and Mrs Sinclair for her to bide her time. One of them may well want to offer afternoon tea herself, and it is just as rude to be too quick and pressing as it is not to offer at all. She was brought up to feel these dilemmas as other people feel pain. She understands Mrs Sinclair's reluctance to impose on them with her shared bathroom and her shared kitchen. Miss Drewery, she realizes, is hardly organized for the undertaking. Yet she hates to leave it until the last minute. It always makes her feel she has taken these words of invitation out of one or the other's mouth.

This park is *their* garden. Any number of small incidents can happen during the hour or so they sit there on their especial bench which was donated by a widow in her will. Mrs Sinclair can be thrust into an unbalanced state of mind by the noises of children or by the look of their inattentive young mothers, while the sight of a young man obviously the worse for drink leads her – as Miss Drewery says – to blow her top. A tramp staggering across the park with his supermarket bag stuffed with newspaper bedding can excite her into raising the disturbing subject of capital punishment.

Most of what they say to each other takes the form of a commentary on what they see. Often it is no more than descriptive or a statement of the obvious. "That boy has climbed to the top of the statue." Mrs Ellison's delivery is not altogether one of complaint, or affront, although her companions accept it as a mixture of both. "There ought to be more park attendants," Mrs Sinclair asserts. Miss Drewery agrees, remembering a previous remark of Mrs Sinclair's to the effect that it is studiously impertinent of the municipal gardeners not to acknowledge her presence from time to time.

It is speculative to say it, but each lady feels she has perceived the glamorous proprieties in the municipal gardens, and that this minor epiphany of a vision of the politics of roses is the climax of their afternoons. Queen Victoria's statue stares across the open field of the park's centre towards Prince Albert who faces her on the other side two hundred yards away. Both figures are seated and Mrs Sinclair sees them in her imagination as at opposite ends of a regal dining-table. Having read a good deal about Queen Victoria, Mrs Ellison is in a position to inform Mrs Sinclair that Prince Albert was long since dead and mourned by the time of life at which Queen Victoria is depicted in the park's statue. It is a point of information she resists bringing out into the open in spite of Mrs Sinclair's verbal rhapsodies. There is a long silence following Mrs Sinclair's flights of fancy in which she then, for her own benefit, envisages a service of silver on the imaginary table, the absolute correctness of the servants, the erect and reliable footmen, a totally dependable butler, and a discreet chamberlain who stoops slightly by Her Majesty's head to whisper that her Prime Minister attends her in the drawing-room on a matter of business most pressing for the well-being of the Empire – childlike but savage India, or General Gordon among the woolly-headed Sudanese, or the feckless and artistic French up to their devious tricks or smudgy oil-paintings.

A conspiratorial hush surrounds their bench. No one who catches sight of them in passing comes away with the impression they seem to be trying to put across – that they own this park, and that it obeys their inclinations and supports their world-views. "The pond just isn't cleaned out as often as it *should*." Miss Drewery agrees while Mrs Ellison says to herself that there is nothing in the slightest wrong with the pond. "It really can have a disgusting *pong*," says Miss Drewery, holding her nose to resonate the word "pong" into the expressive sound she gave it when she was a girl.

Mrs Ellison does not think twice about the small boys with their fishing nets and empty jars that with a bit of luck will become minnows' worlds. To Miss Drewery they are people who will grow up to work in factories and give headaches to the managers she worked for with doting loyalty and brisk runs from office to office and office to mail-room. Or, if they become managers, then they will have grown up to become the sort of people who gave headaches to Miss Drewery and who often failed to offer a lift home from the company's tennis courts at the end of otherwise delightful summer evenings. Her worst memories are of standing alone at bus-stops with her tennis racquet while people she knew drove past her.

If she said anything about these painful recollections to Mrs Sinclair then her companion would remember how she and her husband behaved when they were seated in their imperious little four-door Vauxhall saloon. They had a way of sitting that exuded the pride they felt in being among the very first in the avenue to own a car. Confronted once again with the vexed ethics of offering lifts, Mrs Sinclair would unquestioningly recollect one episode in particular out of several which brought her to the boil at the time. They had been invited to the wedding of her sister-in-law's eldest boy. A couple who lived a few doors along the avenue were close friends of her sister-in-law's husband. They seldom actually *spoke* to this couple although they were civil enough any time they met them on the avenue. It was clear that these people had also been invited to the wedding. It was to be celebrated in a church a few miles away on the other side of the town and afterwards in a hotel in the same district. This other couple had no car. Mrs Sinclair had said to her, "Oh, but of course, *we* shall be making our way in the Vauxhall." "How nice!" the woman said. At first Mrs

Sinclair interpreted the exclamation as a wholly gratifying gesture of joy in Mr Sinclair's car. Later she developed the suspicion that she had been misunderstood, although it was difficult for her to accept that anyone could be so presumptuous as to expect to travel in *her* car when at no time in the past had they received so much as a Christmas card.

In any case, that Saturday, the couple rang the doorbell at the moment when Mrs Sinclair was yelling to her husband that his best cuff-links were where he had left them. It was obvious that a deeply embarrassing mistake had taken place. By then it was too late for the carless couple to arrange for a taxi. In those days taxis were in short supply and it was impossible to get one in less than an hour. It was also far too late to catch a bus and still get there on time. A *change* of buses would in fact be involved. Torn between her own summing-up of the situation as impossible, and Mr Sinclair's constant whining about his cuff-links, she decided to be generous but sullen. There was nothing for it but suffer that pushy pair and hope they didn't expect to return by the same conveyance. What made the whole thing worse was that the man smoked. Not only that, but he talked incessantly of his war experiences with the Royal Corps of Transport. No amount of pointed coughing from Mrs Sinclair in the front seat made the slightest difference.

Mrs Ellison's late husband never owned a car in his life. He simply was not the sort of man who would give up his brisk walks into town. He had been a nervous, careful, disappointed man who kept himself to himself. "He certainly gave very little of himself to *me*." "What's that, my dear?" "What?" "You said something," "Oh, did I?" Mrs Ellison asked, disguising herself to Mrs Sinclair who, unlike Miss Drewery, could never accept that any friends of hers talked to herself.

"Is your son still as keen on his gardening, my dear?" "It's such a long journey," said Mrs Ellison, "and you have to change at Doncaster now."

After about an hour one of them will say, "It's beginning to get a bit chilly." It takes another five minutes before they do anything about it and prepare to leave. It is during these five minutes that Mrs Ellison picks her moment to invite them to stop at her flat for afternoon tea. Mrs Sinclair and Miss Drewery are only too willing. If she doesn't ask, they wonder why not. Mrs Sinclair returns the invitation infrequently and when she does she makes so much fuss about The Complete Strangers that Mrs Ellison ends up by suggesting that her flat, after all, is nearer. Miss Drewery never thinks about invitations. She was uninvited for years. Why should she bother? If they want tea in her flat, then all they have to do is ask. It does not amuse Miss Drewery when Mrs Ellison starts punching her cushions into shape, or when Mrs Sinclair picks things off the floor.

Their afternoons can be devastated by intrusive incidents. Last year, a man, apparently mad, cavorted on the gravel path in front of them and proclaimed himself to be the Acid Evangelist. His hair was long and dirty and his clothes were in that outlandish contemporary style these ladies can hardly be expected to condone. And he had lost a shoe. Mrs Ellison is acutely aware from her reading of her favourite authors that many of life's sensations have passed her by. Long ago she reached the conclusion that she was never intended for them in the first place. But that phrase is engraved on her mind. In spite of the tenacity she once brought to bear on crossword puzzles, it is an expression she has never been able to work out. "What on earth is an Acid Evangelist?" Mrs Sinclair didn't care what it was. "That ridiculous man was wearing *only one shoe!*" Miss Drewery stared after the man's wobbling departure and tried to be tolerant to spite Mrs Sinclair. Clearly, he was not on the managerial staff of anywhere. It was possible, they agreed, that he taught at the university.

A ball lands abruptly among the rose-beds in front of them. A boy climbs the low iron fencing and enters the gardens enthusiastically to get the ball back, egged on by his friends. He asks the old ladies if they've any idea where it fell. They turn away in mournful disgust. Even Mrs Sinclair is temporarily speechless. Mrs Ellison is tempted to be helpful but fights against it, concentrating her mind on the standard set by Mrs Sinclair. Miss Drewery does the same. She wishes she was strong enough to contradict Mrs Sinclair who reminds her of a manager's wife which, indeed, is what she was. How these women distrusted Miss Drewery in her younger, private secretary days, and how insulting the way in which they made it clear, once they had seen her, that they had nothing to worry about. It is an irony she feels now that she spends her afternoons on this unequal footing with managerial widows.

The boy bursts through the rose-beds. His appearance conjures up a picture of low terraced houses of red brick, a father who squanders his dole in the pub, and a mother who does not feed him properly. There is no reason whatsoever why their intuitive summary of the boy should be accurate – in all likelihood, it isn't. Other boys standing by the fence urge him to get a move on. He brushes against the roses as he searches for the ball. Several times he is forced to stop and unpluck himself from rose-thorns. Rose-petals detach and fall. Clusters of them break off and fall to the ground. He finds the ball and throws it to his friends. They run away with the ball at their feet as the boy struggles to unfasten himself from the persistent hooks of the rose-thorns.

Mrs Ellison, Mrs Sinclair and Miss Drewery watch him with horrified fascination. Their roses are so frail and delicate. It is like being told that for technical reasons their annuities have been cancelled. We are deeply sorry, but there has been a dreadful mistake, and your superannuation is all wrong. That unknowing boy looks at them. His expression of innocent pity encourages a tentative but grievously questioning smile to form on Mrs Ellison's face. He stops on the far edge of the rose garden and tugs the last thorn from his pullover.

They sit watching the rose-petals fall. Those that were merely loosened by the boy's presence now fall belatedly to the earth which is already strewn with petals from these poor quality, routinely-administered roses. It seems they will rain on the earth for ever, that there will be no end to it. "It's beginning to get a bit chilly," says Mrs Sinclair. Miss Drewery is saying to herself that she's dying for a cup of tea. Mrs Ellison is reaching a decision – fastidious good manners be damned – that she would prefer to drink her tea alone today. "Would you care to join me for afternoon tea?" she asks.

SOMETHING FOR LITTLE ROBERT

Mrs Mure-Thompson looked at her watch and checked it against the clock on the kitchen wall.

"You really don't have to do this," said Mrs Duncan, her housekeeper, who came in at nine in the morning and left in the early evening.

"If there's nothing I can buy you, when I do so want to give you a present, then please, Letty, no matter what you say, I insist I get something for little Robert." She had a perfunctory way of being pleasant. Mrs Duncan shrugged with resignation and ran the cold-water tap on the cloth she was rinsing. Mrs Mure-Thompson said, "I'm sure he'll enjoy it even if you don't."

"Oh, I didn't mean that. I'm grateful, Madam." It was 1954, in Scotland, and "Madam" was no longer a necessary deferential form of address. But Mrs Duncan found "Mrs Mure-Thompson" a mouthful. It sounded more submissive than "Madam." "It's only that I don't expect a present."

Plump and pale, Mrs Mure-Thompson went from vigour one day to prone uselessness the next. Charities, gardening, and the church might involve her for weeks on end. Suddenly she would cancel all her engagements and withdraw to her room. During these days of brave misery she wrote letters to her many friends in India, where Mr Mure-Thompson had once worked, and in South Africa, Edinburgh, and the Highlands. Mrs Duncan took them to the post. Mrs Mure-Thompson reread the classics of children's literature. She thought of writing a book for children herself.

While Mrs Mure-Thompson was upstairs putting on her coat, Mrs Duncan went into the living room and looked up the long drive for signs of her son, Robert. It was a few minutes past four o'clock, and the school would be out. Robert had been told to come directly from school to the Mure-Thompsons' house. Everyone knew the house, which was much grander than any other house in the district; it had

139

been built just before the war, and looked as if it had reached the age when it could wear the ivy and other climbing plants that covered its white walls. There was no sign of Robert, but there was still time for him to be punctual.

Mrs Mure-Thompson reappeared, pulling on her gloves – her light-blue summer gloves, which conformed with the mild, rainy afternoons of that September, and with its blue evenings. The two women possessed that strength of character known as independence. They knew their minds were confident: Mrs Mure-Thompson in telling Mrs Duncan what to do, and Mrs Duncan in the right way of doing it. That, anyway, was how it looked. Mrs Duncan acquiesced in her role for the sake of her wages. For Mrs Mure-Thompson's benefit, as if out of kindness, Mrs Duncan agreed, without humility, to accept Mrs Mure-Thompson's superiority. She also knew that she was more than a housekeeper. She was almost, but not quite, a companion. She was a hired friend. Only Mrs Mure-Thompson was entitled to any degree of informality in this arrangement. But apart from the "Madam" two or three times a day, Mrs Duncan spoke to her as she would to anyone else.

"That boy," she said. "He walks at the speed of toddle-bonny. And if I know him, he'll turn up looking as if he's walked through a hedge."

"Robert is *very* reliable," said Mrs Mure-Thompson – a flattering contradiction of his mother's opinion of him.

"You can bet your boots on that," said Mrs Duncan. "You can rely on me having to wash his hands and face for a start, before you can take him anywhere."

"Do you think he'd like a sandwich before we go?"

"You'll have little enough time as it is."

They heard scuffing shoes on the gravel path outside the kitchen door. Robert knocked as his mother went to open it. "I thought as much," she said on her way to the sink. She ran the tap and held a flannel under it. "Come over here."

Robert was ten. He stood with his head to one side while his mother wiped his face without taking off his school cap. She left the flannel in his hands for him to wipe them himself while she fetched a towel.

Mrs Mure-Thompson smiled. "If you're quite ready now,"

she said, "then we'll go into town, shall we?" Robert nodded.
"I'll just get the car."

"What kind of coat do you want me to get?" he said to his
mother.

"You'd better leave that to her, son."

"What if you don't like it when we get back?"

"Mrs M-T'll have good taste, son. God knows why, but she
insists on buying us something. Now, you behave yourself.
And don't you go and take advantage of her." Mrs Duncan
buckled and tightened the belt of his navy-blue school
raincoat. She looked down at his socks. She sat back on her
heels, smartening him up. "What have I told you? Keep your
socks *up*." She pulled up the fallen sock.

"The elastic bites my legs."

She wiped dirt from the toes of his shoes with her hand.
Outside, they could hear the cautious exit of Mrs Mure-
Thompson's little car from the garage. "Go on, off with you,
then," she said. She kissed him on the cheek.

It was a fifteen-minute drive into town. "This is where Jim
Hogg crashed his van," the boy said as they approached a
narrow, humpbacked bridge. "Willie Blair says Mrs Hogg'll not
get any money, because Jim Hogg was drunk, as usual."

"Really? Who told you?" she asked. Mrs Mure-Thompson
was interested in the sad controversies of the district.

"Bertie Hogg's in my class."

"How awfully disturbing."

Robert sat up, turned round, and craned a look at the river.
A long raft of small half-sunken metal landing boats had
been left there by the American Army years before. "They say
the Americans forgot to take them home with them."

"Robert, I don't think they actually *forgot*."

"No?"

"No." She laughed.

"You haven't been in bed for a while."

"I've been really quite well, thank you. Quite well." Robert
wondered why she didn't have much of a Scottish accent.
"Touch wood," she said, "but I've been in very good spirits."

"I've had a cold."

"I know, my dear. Did you get the book I sent you?"

"Yes, thank you. I sent you a note."

"Of course you did!" Mrs Mure-Thompson was sincerely embarrassed. "It was very kind of you to write to me."

"I liked it. I really liked it."

"One day," she said, "I'll write one myself. I'm sure I could do it. Do you think I could do one as good? Do you think I could write one as good as *The Little White Horse*?"

Robert had heard his mother talk to his father about Mrs Mure-Thompson's ambition to write a book for children. "Can I read it when you've finished?"

"Will you tell me what you really think of it? Will you give me your honest opinion if I let you read it?"

"I can't read your handwriting," he confessed, remembering the note that had come inside his illness book.

"I'll have you know," she said, "that I can type very well."

Mrs Mure-Thompson negotiated her little car against the kerb in High Street outside Buchanan's Drapers, Haberdashers, and Outfitters. It was a shop that Mrs Duncan did not patronize. "Don't see anything in there you like," he remembered his mother warning his father and himself, "because we can't afford it."

The windows displayed farmerly tweed jackets, sombre suits, and stacked bolts of cloth. Slim imitation ladies, looking a little like young schoolteachers, wore tartan skirts, knitwear, and brown brogues with serrated tongues. One or two wore evening dresses, and one a wedding dress. Rosy-cheeked boys and girls, their waxen knees slightly chipped, advertised the uniform of the school in the town which, Robert had heard, you had to pay to get into if you were not so wonderfully clever that they could hardly refuse you.

They went into the large shop. A boy younger than Robert was sitting on the counter nearest the door and was softly drumming his heels against the dark brown varnish of the counter's wooden front. A woman assistant, wearing the regulation black twin-set and pearls for Buchanan's female staff, was expertly measuring yards of material from a large bolt. She stretched each length of cloth against the polished brass rule inlaid on the edge of the counter. "No. Before you cut it," said the boy's mother, as if about to change her mind, "I'd like to see it in the daylight."

A man approached Robert and Mrs Mure-Thompson, who

had been waiting inside the door as if expecting someone to meet her. "How nice to see you," the man said. He smiled at the boy, suspecting he was the real customer. "It's always a pleasure to see you, Mrs Mure-Thompson. Children's Department?"

"This is Robert," she said, putting her hand on his shoulder, "my housekeeper's son. And he would very much like to see what coats you have."

"Mr Davidson," said the assistant who had been measuring the cloth. Her posture and her voice were aggressively plaintive. "Madam, here, would like to see this in the street, and the bolt's too heavy for me to carry. Would you, please?"

"One moment, Mrs Mure-Thompson." Mr Davidson was displeased. He carried the bolt to the doorway and then, on the customer's instruction, out to the pavement. The assistant behind the counter sighed with late-afternoon exhaustion. "My arms are fair hangin' off," she said to Mrs Mure-Thompson, "what wi' fetchin' an' carryin' bolts of cloth all day. I could do wi' a smoke."

"Yes, thank you. I think I will have this," said the customer to the worn-out assistant as Mr Davidson dumped the heavy bolt back on the counter.

"Sonny, don't kick the counter," Mr Davidson said, discreetly severe, to the bored little boy who was sitting on it. "Mrs Mure-Thompson," he announced, with considerable self-aggrandizement, ushering her towards something much more pleasant than the unwanted interruption he had just taken in his stride.

They tried as many of the coats as would fit Robert. He did not like shopping for clothes. Fortunately, he didn't have to very often; but he hated being asked if things fitted here or were too big there, or if he liked the look of them. This time he found himself entering into the spirit of the occasion.

"Do, please, take the weight off your legs," said Mr Davidson, drawing up a chair for Mrs Mure-Thompson.

"It's tight under my arms." said Robert, without having to be asked.

"I thought so," said Mrs Mure-Thompson. "What about this one?"

"It hasn't any pockets."

143

"Pockets. Yes. What," she asked Mr Davidson, "is a boy's coat if it doesn't have pockets? A coat without pockets is a coat for a little *person*. It is not a coat for a boy. What would he do with his hands? Where would he keep his penknife and his sweeties, Mr Davidson?" She elaborated on this subject until Mr Davidson's professional courtesy ran out of its usual willingness to comply.

"It's quite a popular coat, I assure you. And if nothing else, then at least it wouldn't bag out at the sides with the things boys keep in their pockets."

"Baby rabbits" said Robert, whose confidence was growing.

"What?"

Mrs Mure-Thompson threw her head back and laughed with unexpected pitch. "Yes," she said. "What about his baby rabbits? I'd forgotten all about *them*."

Robert chose a green tweed coat with deerhorn buttons. It had double cuffs, shaped and hemmed in the style of jackets that are worn with kilts. It had deep pockets. It even had a deep inside pocket. "Real tweed," said Mr Davidson, appreciating his wares. He offered a view of the label at the back of the neck. "Without a doubt, this is the real Mackay. And if I may say so," he said, apologetic for raising the subject, "it's excellent value for money." He looked first at Mrs Mure-Thompson and then at Robert. "Try it on again," he said persuasively, helping Robert into its sleeves.

Mr Davidson stood back and appraised the coat with his draper's hypocrisy. He bent down and turned up the hem for Mrs Mure-Thompson to see. "Plenty of room for growth. It wouldn't be one of these coats that'll wear for a year and then you find it's too wee for him." Mr Davidson's head was at Robert's head height. "It's a *lovely* coat. It's just a magnificent wee fit for the boy," he said to Mrs Mure-Thompson as he darted to one side to examine Robert and the coat from what seemed a peculiar angle, the revelations of which were known only to drapers of Mr Davidson's experience. "Oh, yes, it suits you! It suits you down to the ground! Mrs Mure-Thompson, you must agree!"

"Robert?"

"How much is it?" the boy asked. Mrs Mure-Thompson smiled. Mr Davidson laughed.

"It'll be a long time before you have to worry about considerations of *that* nature," said Mr Davidson as he patted Robert on the head. "Will I wrap it up?"

"If it's what you want, Robert?"

"Yes. Thanks very much. I like it."

"On the account?"

"If you would, Mr Davidson."

"Certainly."

While they were waiting in the empty department, Mrs Mure-Thompson beckoned Robert to her chair. He consented to a brief cuddle. "I'm glad you like that coat," she said, "because it's exactly the one I like best, too. Now, isn't that a happy coincidence?"

They went to the front of the shop. "Bye-bye," Robert said to the woman assistant, who was measuring cloth for someone else.

"Oh, cheerio, son," she said, grateful for the unexpected civility.

Mr Davidson presented Robert with his coat tied up in a cardboard box as soon as they reached the door.

It was after five o'clock. The street was busy with traffic. Robert noticed that they walked past Mrs Mure-Thompson's car.

"We're going to the bookshop," she explained. "Do you like Mr Laing's shop?"

"I've never been in it."

"Then I'm sure he'll be absolutely delighted to see you!"

Profuse welcomes met them as they went in the door. Robert's nose was tantalized by the smell of decades of paper. The books that Mrs Mure-Thompson had come to collect were already wrapped and waiting for her. Mr Laing, a thin, ascetic man with drawn cheeks and fair, bushy eyebrows, talked to Mrs Mure-Thompson about the books reviewed in the batch of clippings from newspapers and magazines which she presented to him as her new order. Robert was invited to browse. He did so against his inclination, because he had been warned not to take advantage of Mrs Mure-Thompson, who, when the mood was on her, would buy you anything you had the cheek to ask for or showed any interest in.

"Don't be shy," she said when she joined him among the

books. "Your coat didn't turn out as expensive as I thought it might. Do, please, have them if you want." She coaxed him with a smiling tilt of her head.

"I think my mother would be angry."

"Ah. I see. Well, I'm sure I can smooth things over for you. What did she say to you?"

"She said she'd be angry if I came back with more than a coat." He knew that if he said that his mother had warned him not to take advantage of Mrs Mure-Thompson, then Mrs Mure-Thompson might have cause to be angry herself, probably with both of them. Worse, she might take the coat back.

"I do so much approve of you having these books, Robert. How on earth will you be able to tell me what you think of my own little book if you haven't read these? I'm being quite selfish, you see. I'm not being kind – not in the *slightest*."

"My mum'll skelp me."

"No – no, she won't. I shall *speak* to her."

She took the books to Mr Laing, who wrapped them up. Once again, money did not change hands. Mysteriously, Mrs Mure-Thompson was able to acquire what she wanted without so much as producing a purse, let alone studying the insides of one with that expression of calculating anxiety that Robert's mother adopted when they went to the shops together.

"Well, now that everything's been attended to, we'll make our way home. Shall we?" she asked, as if she were willing to go somewhere else if Robert suggested it.

They drove out of the town. The box with Robert's new coat in it lay at his feet. His three books in their brown-paper parcel sat on his lap. They passed the main gate of the airbase.

"Did you know that the officer in command there is a friend of Mr Mure-Thompson's? Well, he is. He's a very old friend of the family. And one day," she said, "I'll take you to see him. I know how much you like planes. Would you like that?"

"Yes."

They slowed at the humpbacked bridge. They passed a tractor. Robert turned round to see who was driving it. "Jack Anderson's brother," he said. "A horse stood on his foot last year. He had to have an injection."

"The horse," asked Mrs Mure-Thompson, "or Jack Anderson's brother?"

146

"No. Tom Anderson." He wondered at what she had said, and couldn't decide if it was a mistake or stupid. "The horse?"

Mrs Mure-Thompson laughed. She turned carelessly into the B road that led to the village. "It was a joke," she said. "It was just a joke."

She must be enjoying herself, Robert thought.

When they entered the drive to the Mure-Thompson's house, Mr Mure-Thompson's car was already parked outside the front door.

"Now, isn't that just like him?" she said. "How will I be able to put my car in the garage?"

Robert's mother was on the doorstep, with her coat and hat on. They got out of the car. Before anyone could say anything, Mr Mure-Thompson and a guest he had brought home appeared in the garden at the side of the house, strolling and talking. They waved.

"Visitors?" Mrs Mure-Thompson asked, half excited, half disappointed.

"A gentleman from Canada, I believe."

"Oh dear. For dinner?"

"They arrived soon after you left, Madam, so I'd time to do a nice casserole." Mrs Duncan noticed the large, flat box that Robert held under one arm. "And the table's all set. The soup I made earlier's more than ample for a dozen, never mind three."

"What about dessert?" Mrs Mure-Thompson asked.

"There's the sherry trifle I made yesterday, Madam."

"Oh, yes. Quite delicious! I think it must be Mr MacDonald, from the Toronto office," she said, looking at the two men as they strolled across the lawn. "Tonight," she said to Robert, "I shall hear all about Canada, where I've never been. Won't it be exciting?"

"I really must get on now. My man'll be famished."

"We've had such a good afternoon, Letty. Thank you, Robert." She looked towards the lawn and saw that her husband and his guest were walking back to the house. They gave the impression of waiting until Mrs Duncan and Robert had left before joining Mrs Mure-Thompson. She seemed to have forgotten all about the coat. "Thank you, Letty. I honestly don't know what I'd do without you." She seemed anxious to get rid of them. She was looking forward to something else.

Robert and his mother walked quickly down the long drive and then along the road for a bit. "These folk'll be the death o' me, son, what wi' their unexpected guests an' dinners. He didn't so much as phone and let me know there'd be three for dinner." They turned off into a lane. The house they lived in was at the end of it, half a mile away. On either side were high hedges, interspersed with trees. Farther on, cattle nudged up against fences on each side of the lane.

"Green," Robert said. "She bought me a green coat, with horn buttons."

They stopped. "Go on, then. Show me," Mrs Duncan said. She began to untie the string that bound the box tight shut. "To tell you the truth," she said, "I've been scared to ask what it was she bought you. If she said she was buying you a coat, you could've come home wi' very nearly anything." Balancing the box on a raised knee, she took its lid off. "You know, I wasn't very keen on seeing it when she was there, son." She opened the folded tissue that lined the box. "Oh, lovely!"

"That's what the man said."

"What man, son?"

"Mr Davidson, in Buchanan's Drapers."

"Buchanan's Drapers?" She took the coat from the box, laid the box on the grass, and held the coat up to look at. "Lovely," she said as Robert took off his school coat. He slipped into the coat that his mother held for him.

"Tweed. The real Mackay," he said. "That man knows what he's talking about." He pointed to the label inside the neck of the coat. "It says there it's real tweed. See?" he said, holding the neck open so that she could see for herself. "And the hem." He opened the front of the coat. "He said I could wear it for years before it gets too wee for me."

His mother felt the quality of the coat between her fingers. "What's in that parcel?" she asked, noticing it for the first time.

"I couldn't help it. She said she *wanted* me to have them."

"I told you!" She wagged her finger at him.

"I told her you'd be angry, but she said I needed them."

"You told her I'd be angry?"

"Honest, I didn't have a chance," he insisted. "They were in this parcel before I could blink."

He took the coat off, and his mother put it neatly and carefully back in its box. She smoothed the tissue, put the lid on, and tied the strings tight. She put the box under her arm. With her free hand she held Robert's hand. Robert looked at their clenched hands, because her grip was unusually firm. Under his other arm he carried his parcel of books. They walked on together.

"What in God's name will I tell your father? He'll throw a fit when he sees that coat."

Robert had forgotten that his father would be angry. You don't get something for nothing. He had heard him say it before. "I like it," he said, tugging his mother's hand until she stopped in the middle of the lane, in sight of their house. "Make him let me keep it. Please."

EVER LET THE FANCY ROAM

Gavin Fisher is a university bachelor of forty-three who lives in a modest semi-detached house in a university ghetto. His house is cleaned by an elderly woman who has called him "Sir" three mornings a week for the past decade. Fisher replaces his cars every two years, and that, by itself, is enough to isolate him among the more characteristic of his provincial colleagues. Every spare yard of campus concrete is cluttered with their rusting old Saabs, Citroëns, Peugeots, Opels and Volkswagen Campers. Littered inside them is evidence of what, to Gavin Fisher, are their squalid, unpoised lives – partially masticated Galt toys, dummy-tits, "lost" tutorial essays and overdue library books. These specimens of the sub-intellectual, motoring riff-raff are known to Dr Fisher as The Hobbits.

To them, Fisher is a man who patronizes an old-fashioned tailor, who reaps the benefit of an undisclosed private income and who cleans his teeth six times a day. That tumbler on a shelf in his office, with its toothbrush and its tube of toothpaste, has marked him for life in a community which thrives on minor tittle-tattle and major controversies. Know-alls in T-shirts and with the hairstyles of Mesopotamian mathematicians, who populate the philosophy department and are familiar with the thesis of Occam's Razor – *Entia non sunt multiplicanda* – have devised one of their own, which they call Fisher's Toothbrush. For years, however, they, and almost everyone else in that university, have been oblivious to the extent to which Gavin Fisher is, truly, *Doctor Singularis et Invincibilis*.

As usual, Fisher is going to Oxford on Friday afternoon, to spend the weekend as a guest in his friend's College. Valerie, whose thighs will be open to Fisher on Thursday evening, at 9.15 – she has assured him of it – will probably expect him to be present on Saturday and Sunday. Fisher has no intention of sticking around that long: he would as soon miss his Oxford weekends as he would babysit in the university crèche. "Why can't you find a post at Oxford, or Cambridge?" his mother used to say. Although he accepts dinner invitations from his colleagues – not often, but sometimes – it is a lonely life for a man like him who believes, like his Oxford friends, that, socially, his university is a joke. "Isn't it a kind of YMCA with a library? How frightfully *exiled* you must feel!" "Actually," Fisher likes to say in reply, "one shuts one's eyes, and one thinks of England." At local dinner tables, he obeys his own necessity to shine, to be charming, and witty. One of his social responsibilities is to be the best-dressed man in the room. He is under an obligation to flatter his hostess with a politeness to which she is unused. "Isn't he an absolute shit?" the husbands say, when he's gone.

On the other hand, Fisher's frustration is eased by the near-certainty that when X retires from his professorship at provincial Y, the job is as good as his. X was Fisher's tutor at Oxford before the title of Professor contended in X's ambitious mind with all that the city of bells and spires had to offer, and the professorship won. X, too, is nomadic at weekends. Fisher sees quite a lot of X.

Fisher phones X and finds him at home. "Are you going up this weekend?" "Yes, I thought I would." Neither mentions the place. "I was wondering if we might meet." "By all means, Fisher. Absolutely." "Are you free," Fisher suggest, gradually, like a man turning the pages of a crowded diary, "on Saturday evening?" "Yes, I think so," says X. "Actually," says Fisher, "I'll be staying *chez* Mallinder." "I don't want to see *him*, you know." Each chuckles into his telephone. It is a highly satisfactory little call.

Ever since Gertrude, Fisher has had to put up with the not unpleasant thrill of wondering if that floral witch has passed the word among her sisterhood of young female lecturers. "Do you smoke?" he had said, offering his gold cigarette case. "No, and neither will you." He should have taken it as a warning. Still, Rachel from Politics, Ann from Italian, and Tina from Classics have come and gone since Gertrude. Indeed, a university is a hotbed of discretion, Fisher thinks, in spite of its high rate of divorce, its inter-departmental remarriages, its termly scandals, and those married scholars falling for girls and boys. Fisher's affairs last no more than a few weeks. He is brilliant in the technique of preventing his erotic activities from ruining his social life. Husky whispers on the phone, anxiously confessed tenderness, nervous lies, pretences, hinted at, of mysterious complications in his life, these are the nourishment his women thrive on in the first few weeks after he's ditched them. Each affair is a contest of mutual demands, in which Fisher wins. Always at stake, the primary issue, is Fisher's meanly distributed availability. Nothing and no one comes between Fisher and his Oxford weekends.

"What do you mean, not this weekend, you're going away?" Gertrude had been a bit of a shit. "What about me? Where am *I* going?" Fisher explained that he had tried, and tried, but he couldn't wriggle free of it; he was expected, and that was that. "That's what you said last week. This is the third weekend on the trot you've let me down. Why can't I come?" Ghastly tradition, all-male occasion, antediluvian morality, and all that, even in this day and age: Fisher's catalogue petered out in a shrug. "I get it. Yes. The penny drops. Clunk. Right. Go to Oxford." Three weeks, thought Fisher; well, par for the course, although how I got through three weeks of that selfish, egotistical, monosyllabic bitch, I'll never know. "Don't ring me," said Gertrude. "I'll be washing my hair." "I feel so guilty," he said, beginning a speech that no one had failed to listen to before. "I'll be discreet," she said, with a malicious grin. Fisher did not appreciate one bit Gertrude's unruffled tone or the domineering manner in which an armful of Liberty print moved across the table, a hand, like fangs, emanating from her long sleeve, to pat the back of his own as if charitably reassuring him that she would keep her mouth shut. "Mind you," she said, "I'll *have* to be discreet. No one would believe it possible that I could get myself involved with someone who's to the right of the *Daily Telegraph* and wears a suit. For all I know, you probably buy Outspan on purpose and go to church. So you," she warned, with a feminist chirp, "keep your big trap shut, or you'll ruin me."

On many an occasion, lust had agitated Fisher into careless folly, but never before had he felt his mastery of an intimate event slip away from him on such a relentless course that it withered his practised insincerity. "I mean, I'm *fond* of you, *extremely . . . "* he stammered. "You've been through this before," said Gertrude, with a sense of discovery. "Who with?" she asked. "Kiss and tell?" Fisher produced a titter, as if from a hat. Silently reckoning possibilities on her fingers, Gertrude said, "Now I come to think of it, I can remember a few peculiar hellos and how-are-yous. Yes, those little tell-tale looks and glances. What about wives?" Fisher tried to sit back, relax, and fight off a temptation to sink beneath the table or make a break for it. "More wine?" he asked. Gertrude shoved her glass towards him. One thing he would never cease to admire about Gertrude: she could drink like a man. "I've got you," she said, "by the short and curlies. Yes," she said, "you'll keep your mouth shut."

Still, Fisher avoids Gertrude with the same hygienic circumspection with which he keeps at arm's length all left-wing twerps, denim'd radicals, bearers of petitions, Nigerians, sociologists and enthusiastic students of humble origin. It is largely a matter of knowing the shortcuts, the less frequented stairways, of locking his office door and pretending not to be in, of not answering his office telephone. Nor would he be seen dead in the university canteen.

During these quiet, student-free phases of university life, when the fastidious write up their books and no-hopers visit members of the opposite sex in their rooms, or play in rock groups, Fisher is in you-know-where. With four books to his name, he is looked up to by the simple and envied by those bewildered by multiple publishers' refusals. Not a year goes by without Fisher contributing at least once to the better-known of the learned journals. Two or three times a year he reviews something substantial for the *TLS*. Years ago, Fisher observed that it is not what you know, or how well you teach, that counts in the university world. Indeed, he was weaned on that assumption. To make any sort of impression at all you have to get into print and stay there. On one original book a man like Fisher can rely upon being remembered; on four he can be sure that he will never be forgotten, especially if he dines in the right company. It is not a case of "publish or perish". It is "publish and keep publishing, and, above all, *circulate*". Fisher is a tough biscuit; style, he knows, is authority, especially in a provincial hell-hole where style is what they affect to despise. Undergraduates consider it quaint, the way Fisher offers sherry to his tutorial groups at the ends of terms. They notice, too, that as soon as the sherry's poured, he can't wait for them to drink up and get out.

There is something wrong with any young man who enrols at Fisher's university; he is sure of it. To him they look like muscle-shirted bricklayers. Not a year goes by, however, but girl-undergraduates kindle conflagrations of lust in Fisher's hypersensitive loins. Foolish, foolish and dangerous it is, to allow oneself so much as a temporary infatuation with the pretty raw material of one's scholarly profession. Even fantasy can put a chap at risk. Then let that be a rule, he proclaims to himself: no fornication, no Halek, no coitus academicus, no beasting with delicious girl lower-middles from Ealing and Ipswich, Merseyside and everywhere. Aroint thee, wicked scandal!

In spite of the unknown consequences, the hazards which lie in wait for the older man of lust, Fisher is foolish, annually, after the Finals when it is safer, although it is never entirely secure. "And how are the young men of our great Seat of Learning treating you, Miss Smith?" Ah, these hungry giggles! The banter begins several months before the deed. He implants his interest, insinuates it, relying on the principle of selfish competition among girls, that they will keep their naughty deductions to themselves. It leads up to a hand-written memo which they read at the pigeon-holes in the Union. "My dear Miss Smith, Could you pop in and see me? I should so much like to congratulate you on your result." They know what he means.

Anywhere convenient will do. He has skulked in the shrubbery behind the tennis courts at the Women's Hall of Residence, so often he feels he is becoming an expert on botany. He has been in the Women's Hall of Residence, on tiptoe. Fisher has performed in his departmental room with sundry regional beauties, even (he is beyond redemption) in his own house, on the back seat of his car, under the covers on the cricket pitch, breaking his rule.

Were Fisher, by a stroke of good fortune, to find himself permanently established at Oxford, would he . . . ? Yes, he most certainly would. At present he does not, or he does so rarely that it can hardly be said to count, but he has noticed that the very high standard of young lady in Oxford has, if anything, improved over the past two decades of its glorious history. That is one predicament he endures increasingly more often the older he gets. Another is what measures to take should X's professorship fall into his lap, as X has as good as promised it will (well, not quite promised: X has never been candid in his life, and neither for that matter has Fisher). What procedures must he invent to ensure that he gets away with it at provincial Y? Promotion is not going to slap a full stop on his hobby. Since that night, many years ago, when he discovered that women were actually interested in it – "it": it is what Gavin Fisher calls it – his hours of lonely study have been relieved and sweetened, not by female companionship, but by sexual conquest, on beds, in woods, in feminine Minis and 2CVs, on sofas, on the floors and in the baths of these charmingly squalid small flats with their Mucha posters, tights drying in the kitchen, Chianti lamps, coffee mugs, shabby furniture, secondhand cutlery and rows of paper-backs. How he loves their rooms! He is not going to be put off by whatever responsibilities a step up the ladder brings with it.

Valerie Brock. She is a recent addition to the administration personnel. Fisher takes deep breaths as he thinks of her. He rehearses Thursday evening in his mind. Shortly after nine, he will leave his house, and by 9.15 he will park his car, not outside Valerie's flat, but a short distance away. She will answer the doorbell. Fisher will enter bearing two bottles of champagne still cold from his refrigerator. At the sherry party for new staff, Fisher talked to Valerie. It is an occasion he always attends, scouting for new possibilities. Difficult as it was, Fisher treated her as an equal. They met several times afterwards in the course of university life, by, Valerie Brock must think, university coincidence. By the fourth meeting, Fisher was emboldened to break the ice. "Valerie, do you, I mean, do you like sexual pleasure?" Leisurely pronunciation, carefully controlled drawl, naughty smile: "No, no, don't be shocked, please." "I'm not *shocked*, Dr Fisher." "One gets so lonely in a place like this. Our dear colleagues are a shallow, contemptible lot. What do you say? Could we make an evening of it?" "Excuse me, Dr Fisher."

They love the direct approach, Fisher says to Sir Thomas More, frowningly etched, hanging above the mellow wooden trolley on which bottles of drink sit on a silver tray. Notice the brown glint on the cut-glass decanter, a reflection edged with sharp, silver light; and notice, too, Fisher's furniture, those antiques inherited from his mother who used to say, "But *why* can't you get an appointment at Oxford? What *is* keeping you in that beastly place?" Observe, also, these eighteenth-century prints on Fisher's walls in the glow of his mature tables, chairs and bookcases, with not a paperback to intrude among his reputable volumes. There is a dull, establishment effulgence in his rooms, as of the better class of vicarage inserted into a bay-windowed semi-detached house.

Naturally, Fisher says to his full-length mirror in his bedroom, she did not accept that initial, ground-clearing proposition. She said, "Excuse me, Dr Fisher," and went. Have I ever left it at that? No, of course I haven't. I telephoned her in her office and I sent her notes in the internal post. "Look, you mustn't," she said. "I'll tell. I'll scream." "Now, now, my girl, no one actually screams on the telephone. You must give in, Valerie. You really must, you know. Have you any idea of what I'm going through? Please, I'm begging you. Tonight. I *must* see you." "Thursday," she said. "Thursday?" "Yes, Thursday. After nine. But I don't know why I'm doing this." Fisher relished her giggle. "You will, my dear. You will. One need not know. One *does*. Thursday?" "Yes."

In his Shantung lounging pyjamas and Japanese dressing-gown, Fisher descends the stairs, looking like a priest disguised as Noël Coward. After tonging a few pieces of coal into the fire, he settles down with a book. Using a silver propelling pencil, he writes his comments in the margins. Exclamations and question-marks accumulate like neat, vertical litter. His phone rings. It is bad form to answer the telephone too quickly. People might think you are hoping someone will call. "Yes?" he asks peevishly, like a man disturbed. It's Mallinder, his friend whose Oxford college Fisher is to stay in over the weekend. "I was wondering if you could possibly come tomorrow." "I don't know," Fisher says with calculated hesitancy. "Are you teaching?" "As a matter of fact, I am. Actually, it's an engagement on Thursday evening that makes it rather awkward." "Gaboriau is here from Paris. He's terribly keen to meet you, but he's flying on, to Harvard, on Friday." "Gaboriau?" Fisher asks, revealing more enthusiasm than he would have preferred. "Yes. Do try, won't you? And give me a ring, tonight."

Excited by a chance, at last, to meet Gaboriau, and aroused by tomorrow's rendezvous with Valerie's yielded charms, Fisher sits down and endures this antithesis as if it is a pleasantly difficult clue in a crossword puzzle. In more than one Foreword, Fisher has acknowledged his indebtedness to Gaboriau's pioneering studies. Gaboriau is getting on a bit; another opportunity to meet him might not crop up. To be indebted to Gaboriau is one thing; to be known to know the sage is quite another. It has distinct promotional possibilities. How will Valerie take a postponement to, say, Monday evening, after nine? How much, he asks himself, do I *want* to meet Gaboriau? He nods to himself. What am I thinking about? Gaboriau is a *must*! What shall I say to Valerie? How shall I put it? Studying his fingernails, Fisher practises a telephonic speech. He rings her, but it goes unanswered. All right, he says, later. Later will do. He dials Mallinder in Oxford. On Fisher's ear, the ringing-tone sounds different when it's ringing in Oxford. It is like the ringing-tone on the telephone system of another country. Valerie? he says to himself. There are scores of Valeries. Any number of Valeries. There are *always* Valeries. "I've managed to winkle out of my engagement," he says to Mallinder. "It wasn't easy." "Oh good!" says Mallinder. "It'll be a rush," says Fisher. "I can't leave before three, but you should see me about 7.30. It's the best I can do," he says, with the merest suggestion of petulance to encourage Mallinder into believing Fisher is doing him a favour. "And how *is* old Gaboriau?"

FISHERMEN

Wasting my youth on the banks of Dargal Water was not a disagreeable experience. Sometimes, of course, I wish I had squandered myself in dance halls and billiard saloons, but at the time I was the same as everyone else and mad on fishing.

When I was courting my wife, Sophie, it was often along the banks of Dargal Water that we walked. She would come up from Glasgow at weekends, after we had known each other long enough for my parents not to consider that unduly progressive. We would wave to the fishermen, who would return our greetings. These were the fine summer dusks of the nineteen-fifties. Only now do I realize that my friends and neighbours, as they stood there with rod and line, or waded in quick water, expected me to return to them once I had married. Courting and study in another town signified to many of them, in their own amiable and contented ways, absence from the sport of the riverbanks.

I did not return as they expected. Instead, I settled in a city, because the parish I come from already had its dentist, who was a long way from retiring and whose dedication to rod and line made it unlikely he would move elsewhere. Fishing is now a pastime I perform on visits home, and these become rarer and rarer. There is too much to do. My wife sees the place in which I grew up as part of my memory, and therefore visits to my parents are best left to myself. "It's better if you go by yourself," she says. "I'll see your parents when they come to us at Christmas. And you know how you enjoy going out to fish with your brother. You'll spend half your time in the pub, anyway, chattering to your cronies about your childhoods."

My brother and I are not particularly close. David is a year and a half older than I, and yet, to my eyes, to my understanding, he behaves like someone several years younger. He is lean, tall, a constant and expert angler, a competitive golfer, and a bachelor of forty-two. On the other hand, I am short of stature, plump, married, with two children;

and whatever perfections I once showed off with rod and line have disintegrated into the ineptitude of a man from the city. Imagining how my parents see us, as we stow our gear in the back of David's shooting brake before we drive off to the river, I admit we must look fraternal. We must look like old times – two brothers, on good terms with one another, setting off for an evening on Dargal Water. Waving to them as they see us off from the front door is for me one of these moments ripe with the unspectacular significance of our family. I would not miss the moment for anything, although I would much rather that David and I were driving straight to the Plover Inn and that for once he might give the trout a rest.

One evening, a few minutes after we had arrived, we were standing by the bank when John Henderson and Phil McGeoch turned up. They were on their way to the pub after an energetic day's fishing. "Kenneth! Well, well – you're a stranger! How's tricks?" Henderson, who talks like that, was an inseparable of David's and mine when we were younger. He put his hand on my shoulder and looked closely at my face. "You're looking well," he said before he began patting me on the back as if I had swallowed something that wouldn't go down. "Long time no see!" he said enthusiastically, shaking my hand. David looked suspicious of this passionate welcome. I was pleased to see Henderson, but I was not all that pleased. David, I imagined, was wondering if Henderson's delight would take more practical forms – namely, a suggestion that we all go to the pub immediately and have a drink for old times' sake.

"Good to see you," said Phil McGeoch drearily. "Still drilling holes in folks' teeth?" he asked. I had a curious feeling that there was something different about McGeoch's appearance. It was a few years since I'd come across him, but his mouth did not look the same as I remembered it. Probably my efforts to get a closer look were too professional, because McGeoch immediately bared his teeth at me in a way that made it clear he was less than pleased with a new set of dentures. "They don't *fit* me," he said, accusing me and all my fellow practitioners. David was amused at this riverside consultation, but he did not stop his work – lining up his tackle and picking through his boxes of flies and hooks.

"You've been allowed out late tonight," said David.

"I've three fat trout in here," said Henderson, patting his bag. "That'll excuse any drinkie-winkies I get up to."

"She's got you on a short leash?"

"Not at all," said Henderson.

McGeoch looked up at the sound of this lie and then looked at his watch.

"All the best, Kenneth," said Henderson, shaking my hand again. "All the very best. And remember to pop into the Plover if you've a chance."

"Keep up the good work," said McGeoch, with grim sarcasm.

They disappeared along the path and were soon out of sight. "That man McGeoch gets up my nose," said David, passing his line coolly through the eye of a hook. "And Henderson's wife? Talk about punctuality? They say she charges him a fine every time he's late by so much as a minute. She chased him up the street with a bread knife. Did you hear about it? Do you know why?" David laughed as he thought about it.

"No, I haven't heard."

"She sent him into Kilfarran to get their car resprayed." David smirked and chuckled. "A few days later John goes and collects it. He comes home in a blue car. 'Bronze, I said! Bronze, you fool!' She chased him up the street with the bread knife. Didn't give him a chance to explain."

"Explain?"

"The car wasn't ready, so they loaned him another car until the bronze paint was delivered. A bread knife!"

David began walking towards a spot where his experience told him fish were likely to be. A figure called out to us, and as this was Paterson, the bank manager, David was obliged to wait until he arrived. Paterson was out of breath and puffing noisily. His face was as blotched as ever. His nose was scarlet and lumpy. He wore the same tweed hat covered in flies and hooks and was the same caricature of an angler he had always been.

"How *are* you?" He shook my hand vigorously.

"Oh, very well, Mr Paterson."

"Ah, yes. Good. No point in complaining, is there? The

financial institutions have us over a barrel," he said confid-
ingly. "Lovely evening. *Lovely* evening!"

"Mrs Paterson keeping well, I hope?"

"Chirpy. Very chirpy. In the pink. Would you care for a
dram?" he asked in a mischievous whisper.

"If you've got one," I said, pretending to be surprised,
which I wasn't, and looking delighted, which I was.

Paterson produced a hip flask from his fishing bag and
threw off a quick drop himself before passing it to me. There
was nothing in it. Not wanting to embarrass the old man, I
handed it back to him, saying it was just what I needed. He
passed it to David, who struggled with what, clearly, he was
pretending had been a larger gulp of the hard stuff than he
had bargained for. He smacked his lips, sighed, coughed, and
handed the flask back to Paterson.

"Have another," he offered.

"No. That was fine," I said.

"Might see you?" he asked. "Ah, yes, I might see you later,
then, in the Plover."

"We'll be going into the Plover, won't we?"

"We might be," said David, without looking up.

"All the very best for now, then," said Paterson, shaking
my hand once more. "Your wife, I hope, is keeping well?"

"Oh, very well," I said.

"Ah, yes, there will be no dental problems in your family,
Kenneth."

"Aye," said David, "and no money worries in yours, eh, Mr
Paterson?"

The bank manager laughed. "The benefit of a profession,"
he said, "is expert advice to oneself. Well, give my very best to
your wife."

As he walked away, we could hear his puffing and blowing
when he came to the first incline on the path.

"His flask was empty," I said as Paterson, now some way off,
stopped and hoisted back an imaginary dram from his flask.

"I know."

"You pretended."

"You pretended as well," said David. "He took a cure."

"But he was drunk. He's *usually* drunk."

"You're out of touch." David chuckled. "He was kidding on.

One more binge and Paterson's a corpse. Some cure, eh? He gave up everything except the action of his right hand and carrying a flask. Look, I'm getting myself over there before anyone else comes." A few yards away he turned round and said, "Mrs Paterson died three years ago. Or don't you remember? And he hasn't managed the bank for five years. They sacked him. You don't seem to know anything about this place any longer."

For a half hour I stood by myself in the gathering dusk, watching the river, and although I had a line in the water, it was entirely for the sake of keeping up appearances. David, I could see, was engaged in expert casts about two hundred yards from me. His proficiency, the deftness of his movements, even at that distance, gave me the impression that he was ahead of the fish and that he knew more about Dargal Water than they did. As a man of few words, he is suited to the solitude of angling. He looks in harmony with water and weather.

A few moments later I was startled by Bill Jamieson. He had padded up to my back in the soft shoes that he always wears without my knowing he was there until the moment when he cleared his throat. The fright of it almost made me jump in the river. Turning round to recognize him was no improvement, for I had a vague recollection of my mother saying on the telephone that Jamieson had died.

"East, west, hame's best," he whispered, in his gruff, throaty voice. "Now, is that not a fact, young Kenneth?"

"The fish," I said, "still seem a bit on the uncooperative side, even here."

Jamieson looked disapprovingly at my preposterously dangling line. "David," he said, pointing to the indistinct presence of my brother, "takes it seriously." We looked in my brother's direction for a minute or two. The water was darker now. Noises of the stream were louder against the silence of the late dusk. The trees had shaded into dark smudges against the sky, from which the last pink and red were departing. An inevitable greyness was draining the green out of grass and leaves.

"So," said Jamieson, "you're back. They all come back, sooner or later. Your wife with you this time?"

"Not this time, Bill."

"I didn't think so."

"Too busy," I explained, not liking the sound of his remark.

"Och, my wife's the same. Hankers after the big city. Shops and cinemas and all the rest of it. If I don't see you before you go, all the best. All the best," he said vanishing quietly into the growing darkness on his delicately shod paws, a stealthy individual.

For another fifteen minutes I was alone. I sat down and had a smoke. Sound carries on the water at night, of course, and I could hear what I thought was David coughing farther downstream. Realizing it was someone much closer, I stood up and in the dark was bumped into by Dr Fullerton, the minister.

He peered closely at me, and as he recognized me and I recognized him, he burst out with eager greetings. We talked for a few minutes, and then I was aware of how he was standing with his feet apart, shuffling on the path, and a sound of water running into the river. A man of the cloth, I thought, ought to have had the decency to wait until he was no longer in company instead of piddling by someone's side. He sighed and readied himself for more conversation. "My, ye probably don't know it, boy, but you were a landmark in my ministry."

"Me?"

"Forty years've dawdled on by since I dipped your heid in the holy wash-hand basin. Now, am I right?" Dr Fullerton speaks in a homespun version of braid Scots. His humbler parishioners consider it an affectation, while the more respectable consider it a lovable eccentricity, for he comes from one of the best families of Scotland and was educated at Fettes, at the University of St Andrews, and at Balliol College, Oxford. Why he came here is a mystery. "I never forget a baptism, and you were one o' the very furst I ever did. You might even have been the furst o' aw the babbies I've douked in the holy sink." He thrust his feet against the ground, squaring himself up against the evening. "Grand night. It's a *grand* night," he said, grinding the "r" between his teeth as if he meant to remove it from the alphabet once and for all. "You were wedded in my kirk. My, my, birth an' weddin' an' all. An' so the grand design o' the Kirk is carried on. Your wife, Kenneth, is she well?"

"Fine an' dandy," I said, because Dr Fullerton's idiom is catching.

"That's grand. That's *grand*," he said, roaring with a resonance that was louder than his age should have permitted.

"Mrs Fullerton?"

"As is unfortunately well known, son, Mrs Fullerton is a first-rate pain in the neck."

When a man is so disturbingly candid about his wife, there is little you can say in reply – at least to a minister.

"Aye," he said, "but it flows gently, does it not? Well, commune with it while ye've the chance, son. It never changes, but it's aye glad to see ye back, I'm sure. I'll no keep ye, then. The malt's waitin' on me doon-bye in thon Plover, an' as I always say, it's auld enough without me keepin' it waitin' any longer. God bless ye, boy."

By then I'd had enough. Everyone, it seemed, was heading for the Plover except me. I went up the hill to the track where David had parked his shooting brake. David was soon beside me. "This place," he said angrily, "is for fishing. It's a river. My permit cost me money. And it's like a street."

"Did you catch anything?"

"Two."

"Two what?"

"You don't even remember what folk catch in this river."

"Oh, shut up," I said. "You can hardly expect me or anyone else to be as dedicated as you are."

"That's been a wasted night. It was like listening to a wireless down there." He slammed the rear door of the brake.

"It couldn't have been that bad. It didn't stop you catching two," I said.

Before we got into the brake, McGeoch's eldest son and his fiancée strolled past us. "Good evening, Mr Fraser," he said to me. "Good evening," said his girlfriend.

"Oh . . . ah, good evening, Forbes."

"Andrew," my brother whispered.

"Good evening, Andrew," I said, louder.

They strolled on, arm in arm.

"Get that," I said. "Phil McGeoch's son, and he calls me Mr Fraser. That sort of thing puts years on a man."

"As far as he's concerned, you're just as old as his father." He started the engine. He switched on the headlights, which cast yellow beams over the uneven track. I remembered how many times I had seen that before.

"Dad said earlier that he'd see us in the Plover."

"Did he say if he'd drive there?" David asked.

"You don't think he'd walk it?"

"No, you're right. You'll not need me, then."

"What?"

"Early night," he explained. "I've got a long weekend ahead. Golfing."

"Right, then," I said, disappointed. "Suit yourself, but you can let me out at the pub."

"What's up with you now?"

"It's a bit thick, David, standing up your own father. You know how he looks forward to having a drink with the both of us, among all that company."

"You'll be there," he said. "I see Dad every day."

"It's not often he sees us both together," I protested.

"Whose fault is that, then?"

A few minutes later he stopped opposite the Plover. Dr Fullerton was just going in. Before the door swung shut behind him on its slow hinges, I could see my father, Jamieson, Henderson, McGeoch, and several others I recognized. Paterson was sitting on the bench outside the pub, leaning against the wall, cured of drink and with no thirst for it, but irresistibly drawn to his damaging oasis.

"I'll be leaving early," David said as I got out of the brake. "So I probably won't see you in the morning."

"Just one drink. Surely that isn't keeping you back?"

"I'm leaving at five," he said, tapping his watch. "And Kenneth, don't let Dad get carried away in there and drink too much. You drive back."

David's consideration took me by surprise.

"All the best, then. I'll see you next time," I said.

"Sure. All the very best," he said, his hand reaching out across the passenger seat.

A NIGHT OUT AT THE CLUB HARMONICA

It's that time of night, when hunting cats will be getting up off their cushions. It's that time, when cats will be leaving their pampering indoor premises through half-open windows and ingenious cat flaps. Already the early arrivals will have added their luminous watchfulness to the darkness at the top of the wall.

And here I am, being surly at our table, while some somnolent saxophonist improvises on the bandstand; while a half-asleep drummer – dying, I imagine, for a large stiff drink – does his inadequate best to keep up with him, which is more than I can say for the pianist; while a double bass leans like a fat drunk against a wall and its musician has presumably sloped off for a wet or a sandwich.

What is this evening all about? The summer's conversations feel as if they were spoken a decade ago. I keep telling myself I'm not really here; I'm somewhere else, being nice to people, or reading *Le Savon*, by Francis Ponge. I ought to be in bed, plotting to get my hands on a piece of cake without waking my wife and giving her good reason for directing accusations at the growing circumference of my middle. I really ought to be dreaming.

Young fashionables are being loud at the next table. "Cosmeticized angels," I say, "with damaged wings," feeling under an obligation to remark on them if only because my companions seem to be observing them with attitudes that look like ambiguous envy. "Film stars, aristocrats, parasites, and God," I say. "These are the few allowed to have a good time."

My aphorism impresses them like a bad joke. They turn away from the shabby exquisites. I eat an olive. It tastes like a grape injected with petrol.

Fashions appear to have roved backwards again. I can almost hear the sound of far-off propellers and the faint whine of an all-clear. I can see the black market in the waiter's eyes as, eagerly, he obeys my gesture and brings another bottle.

Tonight is all about being able to do that sort of thing. I am a colonel of the Free French, with a pocketful of nylon stockings. Tonight, *chérie*, we will have a good time; a little champagne, some cognac, and your legs will never be the same again.

Tonight, too, is about wanting to stick a carnation in one's teeth and take off in a tango. It is about being different from who you are, in the name of enjoying yourself. For some reason, I want to pretend I am a performing seal. I want to flap my flippers in front of my face, balance a ball on my nose, and catch fish in my teeth. If nothing else, I might change the subject of conversation, which tonight is about opportunities in the antique trade.

Oink! Oink!

No salt-stinking haddocks land on our table; instead, the responsibly chilled wine is delivered in an ice bucket by a starched waiter with the eyes of a lion tamer, who looks steadily at me while I look steadily back at him with the eyes of a mouse. Is it time, I ask myself, for my trick with the tablecloth? I make the offer, but the pianist and the rest of the band, refreshed, break into "Take the 'A' Train" like burglars, and not only do we have to listen to this but we have to watch it.

Is this the post-modernist aesthetic about which I have heard so much this year? Two of us decided, on a large hot day in Yorkshire, that the language can no longer be used to describe anything with clarity. "It is not up to us," I said then. "No," said Charlie. As I looked through the glass of Charlie's new conservatory, I had the distinct sensation of knowing for a fact that his goat, his lawn, the bench under the evergreen, the stalks of last season's Brussels sprouts, the sky, the trees, the stone walls, the moors in the distance – all knew, all *know* where the language is hiding. At one point I felt convinced that Charlie's goat had eaten it. Valedictions all day and every day, but with words like that in it no wonder the language has gone to ground.

A young man, his hair the colour of tadpoles, is putting his tongue into the mouth of a woman old enough to be his mother. "She's old enough to be his mother," says someone's girlfriend at our table, excitedly – but is it with amusement or disapproval?

"Perhaps she *is* his mother," says a friend of mine, and the way he says it makes me glad I didn't get there first. Everyone looks as if words have been stolen from their mouths.

We all look, and imagine we can see family resemblances. But he gives her three ten-pound notes, so we turn away tittering, except me; mesmerized by the expense, I can't keep my eyes off that rakish young man and his elderly consort. "There has to be another explanation," says the girl who started all this. No one else thinks so. Having decided what's going on over there, they are now being urbane. They start arguing about the inflated prices of chinoiserie.

I can hear the sea in the distance murmuring twaddle about the drowned. By now the band is playing something I suspect they are making up as they go along. There are sonic booms over Arcadia and Siberia, over northern Canada, the Antarctic, and the mid-oceans, which no one ever hears. There are times when I feel like the ubiquitous decimal in a computer. I want someone to write "I LOVE YOU" in lipstick on the back of my white tuxedo. But I haven't got a tuxedo.

Eavesdropping, I can just catch what some bearded little charlatan is saying about his forthcoming *plaquette* of verses. I want to go up to the microphone and announce that Paul Éluard, the twerp's mentor, whom he is supposed to have visited earlier this summer at Vence, has been dead since 1952.

A drunk blonde, singing, is fighting her way to the microphone. How embarrassing for her husband, who is reaching up to hand money to the pianist. Instead of a tipsy discourse on women's underwear in the twentieth century, from the feminist-Presbyterian point of view, which was too much to hope for, she implicates herself with "Boulevard of Broken Dreams". I am so determined to applaud this *veritas* that I am applauding already, as if applauding my determination, and she's just started. Yes, I see; I understand why the large party she is with is looking at me like that. She must be popular if her friends, in spite of her inebriated squeaks, think of my standup vigorous handclapping as impertinent criticism.

In the men's room I want to tell the man standing next to me that the language is sound asleep or dead or that, conceivably, Charlie's goat has eaten it; and that even in remote places the wilderness is dying. But I tell this to the urinal, and bark at the stranger. In return, he strikes me viciously with his fist, straight against the source of my bark. He must have a soft fist – my mouth is not bleeding.

Woodsmoke, cicadas; no, true enough, I'm not here at all. I am in the *salle d'attente* at the Gare d'Austerlitz on my way toward woodsmoke and cicadas, and it is past 2 a.m. Policemen and ticket inspectors are staring down the beams of their torches. There is the sound of feeble snoring, as down-on-their-luck *voyageurs* wait out the night in an ashtray. No, nowhere in particular. When I reach Corrèze if I ever do, I suppose the fragrance of the countryside will smell of my disillusionment like that sweaty waiting room, or this night club that tastes of cigars, cigarettes, wine, and everything that's on the menu. When I shut my eyes, I don't know where I am. Trees in the night club, the saxophonist swaying like a deep-sea diver, the drummer carried away on his own furies. Tame owl on my shoulder, what time is it? No, no, I am in the wrong bed, that's not her book under the pillow.

Coupledom. I hold somebody's hand for the sake of appearances. Much has been done for the sake of keeping up appearances – fidelity, infidelity, good manners, mass murder. It is the wrong hand. I slap my own hand and pick up another hand from the table. "What is this," I ask, "a séance?" Moonlight is turning to char on the high heather fields five hundred miles away. "Why are you holding my hand? Give me one good reason why you should, and you can hold my hand," she says.

"Because," I say, "I'm dishonest."

"And what of your big mouth? Can you keep it shut?"

Discretion, I tell her, is an art in which I have taken several crash courses.

The summer is turning to ice in the head of my friend on my other side. "I don't feel married," he confesses. "I feel undivorced."

"The grass," I tell him, "is brown, black, purple, any shade you like, but it is never green, let alone greener, on the other side of the hill. Grass, friend, is grass."

"Thank you," he says. "You are so helpful."

169

"At thirty," comes a braying voice from the distance of a far table, "she became something of a bargain, frankly."

Oink! Oink!

Another bottle in an ice bucket.

"'I let go of life with my gloves on!'"

She tells me to sit down, and I discover that – true enough – I'm standing up. Making the most of this, I explain that I'm playing my favourite game, which I call Hunt the Idiot. She turns away from me. Perhaps she's trying to tell me something. They all tell me to sit down. Seated, I close my eyes, and see things. Lacking the courage to be a performing seal, I could leap up on to the bandstand and make an announcement. "Ladies and gentlemen! I am thoroughly browned off with the entire universe!" Many people have done that; I am sure of it. They probably survived to live down the humiliation and tell the tale. But what I feel to be absolutely necessary is a gesture that, before these friends of mine, will not be misinterpreted as a cry for help but understood as an insult. In years to come, I will wake up in the middle of the night, chewing the pillow in apocalyptic embarrassment.

That waiter, the one with the eyes of a tout, has selected me as the likeliest source of his tip. The cheek of it! From what evidence has he sized me up as someone cowardly with his generosity? Why me?

Oink! Oink!

"Come and get it!" shouts the mouse to the lion tamer.

Time now, I think, for my trick with the tablecloth.